Smokey Hollow:
The Shoe Box Coffin

David Mack-Hardiman

Designer: Rachel Bridges
Editor: Julia Lavarnway

Publisher: Museum of disABILITY History

ISBN: 978-0-9977740-3-0
Library of Congress Control Number: 2017948741

People Ink Press
in association with the
Museum of disABILITY History
3826 Main Street
Buffalo, New York 14226

PEOPLE INK PRESS

The language which may have been used during this time period has been replicated in this fictional account. No offense is intended toward any individual or group.

DEDICATION

In memory of my beloved parents,
Richard and Anne Waterman Hardiman

CHAPTER ONE

Upon my graduation from high school, my father announced over a dinner of savory pot roast and coconut cream pie that from now on he would be collecting rent from me each week. I was suddenly inspired with some much needed motivation to look for work. My Uncle Willie had mentioned that they were looking for people to do yard work at Smokey Hollow, a hospital of sorts in the Allegheny Mountains. In a small town, just as a creek becomes a crick, so a hollow becomes a holler. Carved into a mountainside, Smokey Holler was surrounded by a mauve sandstone wall, so it was difficult to see from the town below. It was formerly an asylum of some kind, and there was talk in town about a few unfortunate patients who had tried to escape. Apparently, they didn't know that there was nothing on the other side of the wall except pine trees and certain death. Or maybe they did.

I rang up Smokey Holler and spoke with a woman whose name was Juanita Lyons. She politely scheduled a time for an interview and told me how to get to the facility. The night before my interview, I went out with a few of my high school friends. I decided to feed them the fodder and told them I had an interview at Smokey Holler. Once the snorting and hooting died down, they made a long string of remarks about how "the bin on the hill was the perfect place" for me. My friend Donnie Wayne Briggs began his predictable litany of rescue squad tales, passed down by his Dad who volunteered with the fire department. He told us that one person jumped off the wall and landed in a tree. It was deep winter, and the person likely froze to death there. Because of the rugged terrain, the only method of retrieval was to cut the tree down. However, the vibration of the chainsaw shook the body loose, and it shimmied its way down the gigantic pine tree. Commander Briggs was nearly struck down by this unfortunate soul. In every story, Commander Briggs is just inches away from mayhem and danger. Yarns and fish stories are spun into surprising authenticity in rural America. Donnie Wayne also told me the sad story of Eddie Le Clair. He scaled the wall and realized when he reached the top that he needed to go back into the Holler. While trying to get back down the wall, Eddie fell and cracked his skull on a rusty piece of farm equipment. He bled out before anyone noticed he was missing. Donnie Wayne went on with other cryptic tales of ghosts. As the night wore on, his stories wore on me, and I decided to head home.

The following morning, I hopped on my ten–speed after a quick breakfast of peanut butter toast and tomato juice. I raced through town and headed into the woods to find Asylum Road. Thick fog permeated the air, and I soon realized why the vapor was referred to as smoke. This was the hollow, the flat and lonely territory between the mountains. I worked my way through the piney forest, using all my gears to get up the hillside. Trying to flip my cassette tape in my Walkman, I took my eyes off the road momentarily. Hitting a patch of loose gravel, my bike slid and toppled over. I yelled a few good curse words! I scraped my elbow through my button-down shirt and felt a trickle of warm blood oozing out. My foot caught the chain and pulled it off. To add insult to injury, my cassette player was strewn about in pieces. Although angry, I also became anxious. I was sweating and felt my heart start to race. This was a fine mess. I pressed my elbow into the bike seat to stop the bleeding. Then I sat down to fix the chain. You know how it goes when you try to put the chain back on. Just as you successfully get it back on a few of the sprocket teeth, it falls off a few of the others. This can go on for way too long.

Once I had my bicycle back in shape, I hopped back on. I looked ahead at the road, only to see a car slinking along toward me at a slow rate of speed. It crept along over the gravel. I noticed that it had an old-fashioned gumball on top, and it looked like an ancient ambulance. I swung my leg back off the bike and put the kickstand down as the car closed in on me. A man who was hiding behind excessively large sunglasses and a handlebar mustache startled me as he clicked on a megaphone. His hands were shaking and cyanotic. He shouted, "private property!"

The volume gave me a partial panic attack. I began nervously wobbling on the bike and couldn't hook a flowing stride on the pedals. I said, "I am here for an interview."

This skinny little man resembled a cross between Festus from *Gunsmoke* and Barney Fife. He was like a caricature of that law and order man who never should have been issued a gun. With one hand on the wheel, he fumbled with the megaphone but couldn't get it to work.

He tossed it across the vinyl seat.

He croaked in a much feebler voice, "I said, private property!"

"I said that I am here for an interview."

He looked over the top of his sunglasses with sad, lonely eyes.

"An interview? Is your interview for work or to be admitted?"

He started laughing at his own "joke." He chuckled his way into a mucous spasm and the resulting uncontrollable cough of a long-term smoker. Without apology, he spat right out the window toward my feet.

"I am here for an interview with Juanita Lyons."

"Well then why are you dressed for church?," he jeered with an eye on my tie.

This was the second insult. I got back on the bike and slowly set off up the hill. Idly, he followed me, driving with one hand and smoking with the other. Morning fog gave way to summer sun, and I began to sweat heavily. Where I once was pretty spiffed up, I was now sweaty with a blood-stained shirt and black oil on my hands.

Smokey Hollow was a sprawling complex with a large administration building in the center sitting beneath two towering oak trees. Some of the outer buildings appeared deserted with boarded doors and dangling shingles on the roofs. Weeds and untamed bushes grew near the abandoned sections. Serpentine ivy vines wound around the buildings and through broken windows. I stashed my bicycle outside the administration building and went in to find Juanita. Mesmerized by the marble foyer, I found her office after a few minutes of exploration. Sometimes, I would get intrigued by nature and architecture and just sort of wander like that. My father had referred to them as "seizures" and fairly frequently suggested that I see a doctor about them. Oddly, no appointment had ever been made to help solve my malady, so I guess the threat that I may need to see a doctor was the intended cure. Juanita asked me some fairly routine questions, and I signed the typical forms. She announced that everything seemed to be in order and that I should report back the following morning. I assumed that all this meant that I had been hired! As the interview wrapped up, she read a prepared statement from some sort of dog-eared binder: "As some of the most unfortunate people here have relatives in town, the care and treatment they receive here should remain confidential. Their families have suffered enough and should be spared further upset or embarrassment." She tersely dispatched me to the security office to have my ID card prepared. The name on the office window read "Officer Elmer Muskie." And, there he was, the same person who had followed me up the hill in his creepy car. He giggled with adolescent, bullying mockery.

"So, our choir boy will be mowing lawns tomorrow, eh?"

I withdrew and stated flatly, "I am here to pick up an ID badge."

I guess he didn't like that too much because he began a long-winded recitation of rules. I was not to share my badge or deface it in any way. No one was to enter the grounds while using my badge. He blathered on and on.

Just then, we were interrupted by a tall, red-headed man in worn and soiled work clothes. His hands were dirty, but unlike everyone else, he smiled faintly. He shook my hand.

"H-h-hi. I'm D-D-Dan McRae."

The security guard completely ignored the greeting and continued to recite rules, even louder and more emphatically. Dan backed off and retreated as Officer Muskie continued his lecture. Dan took me to the maintenance barn after I got my ID badge.

"J-j-just so you kn-kn-know, I stutter. We call him M-M-Musty 'cause he stinks like a wet cellar. M-m-mind yourself around him."

After the Musty in-service, my ride downhill was much easier! I finally felt free again! I took off my ridiculous tie and cruised wildly down the mountainside. It seemed that work, church, and school were tense enough and that tying a noose around one's neck just made it all that much worse. Thankfully, I could mow lawns in jeans.

Our family dinner of sumptuous chicken à la King and biscuits was full of teenage tension and parental flapdoodle. I had waited longingly for this meal, drooling like a dog when I smelled the rolls. My mother referred to the biscuits as one of her, "secret recipes," but we all knew that they came out of a tube. Sadly insistent that they were her creations, she went to great lengths to hide them in the vegetable crisper and whack the tube in the bathroom so that we would believe this delusion. I like it when people are so obvious with their ridiculous stories. It was funny, in a way, to think of all of her criticisms while just wanting to call her out on her flakey little pastry lie. But these transgressions are sometimes best saved for the future, as we accumulate ammunition along the way.

At dinner, Mom and Dad rotated like a tag-team.

"Now, I see you have ruined the only decent dress shirt that you owned. You'll have to save for a new one. Those raggedy concert tee shirts that you wear are not going to be acceptable at church."

I began to squirm in my seat. My comforting foot-jiggling fired up. Dad gulped down some milk and joined in the fun.

"It is going to be difficult to save anything on that paltry salary at Smokey Hollow. But you best get over to the bank and open a savings account, just in case you are able to save something for your future. Of course, college may not be in your future given some of those crummy grades that you got this year."

My sisters, Rita and Colleen, sat sullen and morose, waiting for their latest lecture.

Mom looked down at her congealing à la King and began berating my sisters.

"I thought you might have gotten some formal wear when you two went out shopping. From what I can see, everything is denim. In my day, denim was worn by farm people. And Colleen, that Gypsy jewelry you favor makes us look like we are from the other side of the tracks."

"The other side of the tracks? What exactly does that mean, Mother? Is the railroad line somehow the divider between good and evil? Is it heaven on our side and hell on the Gypsy side? When was the last time you saw a Gypsy in this backwater town, anyway? They have better taste than that."

My father was suddenly engaged and appeared to have a surge in blood pressure. Veins throbbed in his temples.

"Young lady, you need to respect your parents! No daughters of mine are going to be parading around town like Gypsies or burlesque dancers."

At that point, I choked. Actually, I pretended to choke so that they didn't know that I was laughing. My ruse was effective. Rita and Colleen were already on their way into the kitchen. Colleen turned and winked at me her approval as my mother asked if I was okay for the eleventh time. After some television time, I retired early so I would be ready to roll in the morning.

CHAPTER TWO

Morning came with mom pounding on my bedroom door unnecessarily while I watched television and slurped cereal in the living room. Once she figured out that I had managed to awaken without intervention, she reminded me to stay out of the sun and avoid touching strange plants in the woods. She had made me a lunch and had put out a hat for me to take. I envisioned myself sunburned to a crisp, wandering through the woods to find strange plants to touch and laughed. I grabbed the lunch on the way out the door. The hat was not quite the baseball cap I expected. It was about three feet across and reminded me of a hat an elderly grandmother would wear. I hid it in the garage as I hopped onto my bicycle.

My first few days on the grounds of Smokey Hollow were long but not particularly challenging. Dan loved chewing on foxtail weeds, so he was always on the lookout for them. I soon found this habit to be addicting myself. He had taught me to go to the farthest point on the property in the morning so it would take longer to get back and forth for breaks. He showed me poison ivy and oak so that I would recognize them on the grounds. While Dan was somewhat socially withdrawn, he knew a great deal about the world around him. He instantly recognized varieties of trees and shrubs. Like a human barometer, he felt changes in the weather and accurately predicted storms. He watched the clouds intensely and always knew the direction of the wind. And, all the while, he stammered, struggling to get his words started. I got used to it fairly quickly. Somehow, what he had to say seemed more important because he put so much effort into producing the words.

"That there is a b-b-b-urnin' bush. It is in the B-B-B-ible. In the fall, the l-l-leaves look like they is on f-f-fire before they drop."

On rainy days, we would work in the greenhouse where many plants were grown. There was a large garden on the property that needed weeding as well. It was there that I first saw some of the Smokey Hollow patients. Despite all that I had heard, some of them seemed quite capable and friendly.

One gentleman, Henry, worked diligently pulling weeds. Hourly, he would ask to smoke his pipe and the staff person would dutifully dole out the tobacco and light it up. After a few intense, red-faced drags, he would break out into spiritual songs. The earth seemed to tremble a bit underneath as his voice soared and bellowed. He held his eyes tightly shut whenever he sang, as if he were transported elsewhere. Sometimes, I would grab a cigarette break while he sang. Henry could be somewhat impatient, and he seemed to like the structure of his routines. Once the worker forgot his tobacco at the ward and had to go back and fetch it. Henry was swearing and spitting in a rage, so I emptied a cigarette into his pipe to tide him over. One day, we saw a dragonfly as we took our break. I pointed it out to him. He said, "my brother Homer loved dragonflies." When I asked where his brother lived he said, "Satan took him to heaven in the fire." I don't remember what I said in response to that. It is possible that I said nothing at all as I didn't know what he meant.

Some of the folks shuffled along slowly. One older woman seemed to be in a perpetual state of motion. Her face twitched and her hands shook repeatedly. I asked Dan what he thought was wrong with her but misheard him. I thought he said that she had TB but he later corrected that to TD. He said that it was caused by taking certain medications for years. While she was apparently calmer, she looked sadly uncomfortable in all activities. She appeared as if she might jump out of her own skin.

One day, as we were weeding, I showed the group some milkweed plants. One resident seemed enthralled by them. I opened the sticky shells to unveil the feathery seeds. The tiny, cottony parachutes drifted through the air, searching for a new home. Each time she blew them away, she smiled ear to ear and rocked back and forth. She clapped when we were done.

As Dan and I finished getting the mowers ready one morning, Musty cruised up in his creeper car. He drove along in his sinister style and whipped a cigarette out into the grass. Not realizing that we had just been gassing up the mowers, Musty started a small fire, which erupted with a thumping sound. Dan quickly grabbed a nearby hose and soaked down the area. The chief of security rode away while laughing. I told Dan that he should report this, as Musty could have set the whole place on fire.

"R-r-r-eport it to who? If you see a snake in the g-g-g-rass, there ain't no reason to p-p-poke it with a stick. S-s-stop getting all worked up! Musty is in c-c-cahoots with the director, Steiner. Leave the s-s-snake alone!"

Autumn came early to the mountains. My parents dragged a reluctant Rita and me to a ham and squash supper at the church one evening. Every item of food tasted as if it had been boiled for weeks. Colleen had claimed that she was going to be working at the "Meat-n-Taters Diner" but she was likely lying again. Colleen was able to lie freely, and my parents either missed it or ignored it. Rita and I were bored and tried to come up with an exit strategy. Before dessert was served, I was cornered by Miss Verna Lou Vaughn. Verna Lou was spewing on about Satan's influence in music and films while she spit her food with venomous accuracy. There is nothing quite like a little fire and brimstone ham spittle to ruin your appetite for dessert! Rita said that she couldn't remember if she fed our dog, Jelly Beans. She wasn't overtly lying, which helped soften up the parents a bit. Dad reminded us not to appear disrespectful as we quickly made our way to the door.

Once we hit the chilly air, we fired up some smokes and cursed. We walked quickly down the woodsy path between the Raccoon River and the railroad tracks. I told Rita that Verna Lou was like the last fly of the summer, droning on but unable to be drowned out. We laughed when I told her that the church elder told me that Satan lived "in the salacious humor of *Laugh-In*"!

Rita laughed and chimed in.

"How about the Lumpkin Family Gospel Singers? I guess I should feel sorry for their poor children, but it took everything I had not to laugh. Lonely Lena Lumpkin, praising away with her eyes cast on heaven!"

Up at Smokey Hollow, Dan took me aside one day while I was raking leaves. He said that it was likely that my work with him would be ending soon. He had put in a good word for me with Juanita Lyons, and she said that there were some openings in tending the patients in the wards. I thanked him but said that I would probably be hitch-hiking to a warmer climate in the South. Actually, I made that up but I didn't want to seem like I needed to stay there. My rake caught the corner of a small stone in the ground. I bent down to free it and noticed that there was a smudged number on the rectangular stone. I asked Dan what it was, and he told me that we were standing in the middle of the Smokey Hollow cemetery.

"These here is the indigents and the f-f-families didn't come claim them when they died. Some of them are older g-g-graves, from when it was the asylum. Over there are some of the n-n-newer ones. Dr. Steiner says that most of the d-d-disabled folks die young. I had to b-b-bury a few kids who had mongolism, and a c-c-couple who choked to death."

This was grim. Bricks and numbers! This was unfair and ridiculous! I started to get worked up about it, and Dan said, "S-s-simmer down! It ain't right, but you don't n-n-need to throw a r-r-rock at a mad dog every d-d-day of your life."

Meatloaf was one of my favorite foods. Mom had perfected a ketchup crust on top with juicy green peppers running the length of the loaf. Between them sat a crispy slice of bacon, burnt to perfection, all of which was accompanied by peas and mashed potatoes. Over this meal, I announced to my family that I would likely be working in one of the wards at Smokey Hollow.

My mother chimed in. "Oh my, a career now as some sort of babysitter?"

Her soulmate added, "Well, he is lucky to find any kind of job. He daydreamed through half of his schooling anyway. Always was something a little odd about this one."

My foot began involuntarily wiggling. I pulled back one of my cuticles. I had always preferred to bite them until they bled, but I knew that this would not be tolerated "at the dinner table."

"Have you ever listened to any of these dumb little dinner conversations, Dad? I would rather be odd than be sitting here at all."

"Oh, here we go again now with your sarcasm, young man! You are not going to get anywhere in this world with your disrespect. Honestly, my children spend a good portion of their days ridiculing people in authority with insults and wisecracks. I am out slaving away at the office every day and you little know-it-alls make minimum wage. When you get a decent job, let me know. In the meantime, clam up!"

Mom added, "You children should spend more time with those nice Lumpkin kids. They have wonderful grades and sing like angels in church. They seem like wonderful role models."

Colleen suddenly said she felt faint and that a migraine was coming on. The stormy clinking of silverware, our family dinner bell, signaled that the meal had ended. My anger mingled with the uneasy meatloaf taste in my mouth, and I was furious that such a potentially good meal had become such toxic, unsavory acidity.

The next day I met with Juanita Lyons. Mousey and somewhat frail, Miss Lyons had a sad air about her. She asked me a few questions and mentioned that Dan had given me a good reference. She said that the institution was short staffed in some of the, "low grade wards." She used the intercom to page Mr. Muskie. I told her that I knew where the ward was, but she insisted that I needed an official escort. In came Musty. Apparently, he wore his reflector sunglasses indoors.

"Well, I see you are moving from moving dirt to changing diapers. Congratulations!"

I mumbled something inaudible as I felt my temples pulsate.

"You are going to have to learn how to communicate if you are going to be working here. Sounds like you have been spending a little too much with your friend Dan."

Musty told me that I needed to ride along with him to the ward. Mercifully, it wasn't far away. The ride was unspeakably awkward. The "security wagon" reeked of cheap after-shave, old tobacco, and the funk of unwashed hair. Low slung on the greasy seats, I felt like a creep as Musty slowly moved along, his head rotating like an owl whenever he saw anyone. When we got to the ward, he grabbed a huge ring of keys that was dangling on the dashboard.

As Musty began unlocking doors, I started feeling a tad nervous. I really had no idea what to expect at all. The security guard was of no help, as usual.

"You don't seem cut out for being an attendant here. You are going to have to toughen up."

My heart started to race. I saw a grizzled attendant sloppily piling up bags of laundry on a loading dock. At last, Musty unlocked the last door. I felt an immediate sensory overload. The patients seemed to be all children, and several were moaning or crying. There was an overpowering odor of some sort of cleaning fluid weakly competing with the fetor of confined human beings. I was stunned to think that I had never seen these people outside and wondered how often they left this room. For once, Musty made a hasty retreat, and I stood in the center of the room, choking on my own fear. A dark-haired woman approached me and introduced herself as Birdie. She invited me into an office area. Between an overflowing ashtray and some cold coffee, I sat in an uncomfortable folding chair. Birdie had striking features and a calm, reassuring demeanor. She said that it was alright to have a case of the jitters on the first day. She said that she had been working on the ward for seven years, so I relaxed slightly.

"As a young girl on the reservation, I took care of my sister who had polio. I have always taken care of people who were crippled or slow. Mind yourself around the afternoon supervisor, Velmajean Sanders. She is unpolished and rough-hewn. She hangs around Musty, and they feed information to Superintendent Steiner. There ain't no difference between any of them. They are bottom feeders, down with the carp and the crawdads."

Birdie took me through the ward, pausing at each child to let me see the kids she had mentioned earlier. She explained that Smokey Hollow was an adult care home and that if the state came calling, the kids would be moved temporarily.

"They ain't certified to take in these young ones, but Steiner told us that no one wants them and we should do our moral duty to care for them. The good doctor must be getting some money for the kids because he doesn't provide any of his care for free."

I met Vina Howard, a small, blonde-haired girl who was humming and twirling in circles.

"We think she has the autism. They ain't real social and like to do their own thing."

The external door opened, and a grizzled-looking attendant wheeled in a cart loaded with covered trays. Vina folded her ears down and ran into a corner. The rusted-looking cart squeaked and squealed its way through the room.

"Grub time," the attendant moaned with disinterest and disgust. Birdie asked me if I could feed Vina and Gary, a young boy who was positioned in an antiquated-looking wheelchair. She said that Vina would pretty much eat on her own as she handed me a special spoon to use with Gary. I didn't know the specifics of his condition, but I assumed that he couldn't use his arms. I grabbed two trays and put them on a table. Vina gravitated over, and I brought Gary closer. He opened his mouth, so I filled the spoon for him. I had no idea what I was feeding him. It resembled mashed potatoes with peas or something similar. Gary seemed receptive to the unknown substance. I found a stack of clean towels (which in retrospect may have been clean diapers) because Gary was dribbling out a fair amount of what I was putting in. I fashioned a bib of sorts for him so that everything didn't go directly on his shirt. Vina took care of her lunch at a fairly rapid pace. I asked her to slow down a bit, but she did not and finished her meal. She left immediately, back to her twirling station. With Gary, lunch was quite a bit longer, but I managed to get it all done safely and breathed a little sigh of relief.

A few days into my work on the ward, I met Velmajean, the afternoon matron. She looked like unoiled leather, and her eyebrows were penciled in. There was no formal introduction. She walked up to me and chimed in.

"Watch you don't get too attached to them here. Those that don't go up to the graveyard will wind up in other wards. You ain't workin' here to get all cozy with them. Ain't no one who wanted them, even their own parents. Dr. Steiner is the only one who would take them in. We have one of the lower grade girls coming back to help with the kids starting next week. She don't know how to do much more than rock in a chair, but it helps put the poor babies to sleep when they are agitated. You are goin' to have to watch her so she don't run off and make sure she ain't feeding them. She ain't staff!"

CHAPTER THREE

One chilly evening while Dad was out of town on business, Mom made lasagna. It tasted acidy and was absent of spice. Mom blamed it on spoiled cheese from overseas. Colleen, who had spent a lot of time at the home of her boyfriend, said, "I think you are supposed to use tomato sauce, not all tomato paste. Mrs. DiStefano uses garlic and oregano." And with that, the horses were out of the gates.

"Well, why don't you all go over to their house for dinner? I doubt there would be anywhere to sit with all those kids and the grandparents from the old country."

"Maybe we will," Colleen shot back. "The grandparents are sweet and call me bambina."

"Well, heaven knows what that means! I have read that eating too much garlic can cause women to sprout facial hair, so you had better watch whatever you are eating over there."

"Oh my God! What are you talking about now, Mom? Did you read that while you were waiting over at your little hair-coloring salon?"

"You children have wise little mouths and wild ideas. I wish you would take some lessons from that Lumpkin family. The children are so devoted to their parents and their studies."

Not missing a beat, Colleen said, "And, they are major league dorks. They don't even own a television!"

"That's it! You kids have ruined another meal and are taking advantage of your father's absence."

Mercifully, Mom started a short speech about unappreciative children. While pretending to cry, she wiped her napkin on her face, unknowingly leaving a string of tomato paste on her cheek. With that, her lasagna stigmata, she left and slammed the bedroom door behind her.

Colleen dropped me off at work the next day because there had been a little snow overnight. She declared that she had no idea how I could work at Smokey Hollow, but she thought that it was cool anyway. She said that she had to go to work slinging hash to the truckers, and I suddenly felt sorry for her. While I was truly beginning to appreciate my work, she hated hers.

I went into the ward and heard a rhythmic creaking sound. I noticed that someone was hunched over in the rocking chair, holding a child. They rocked back and forth, over and over again. Birdie took me over and introduced me to Polly, who had jet-black hair. Her head was slender and sloped more than most. Her teeth protruded a bit. She smiled easily and profusely and seemed transfixed by the motion of the chair. When she smiled, I realized that I had met her when we were out gardening in the summer. She loved the milkweed! The child, whose name was Bambilyn, seemed to be in a hypnotic state of happiness, her body lolling about while her eyes rolled back and forth. This went on for a good hour or so. Polly rocked like a whirling dervish in a perfect circular pattern. As she threw herself forward and back, the chair rotated slightly to the right every time.

At last, with Bambilyn fast asleep, Polly slowed the chair down to a crawl. Birdie took "Bambi," as she was known, to her crib. I asked Polly if she had a license to operate the chair. While I wasn't sure if she understood what I said, she flashed her ear to ear smile and clapped her hands together. I liked her. She sat with me when I fed Vina and Gary. Polly had her own tray and assertively handed me items when she needed them opened. She would plop them in my hand and smile. When the ward settled down for a medication induced nap after lunch, I asked Birdie if Polly could talk.

"Only word I have ever heard is 'ouch' when she is hurt!"

Suddenly, the ward door opened brusquely and in marched Velmajean.

"Well, it is snowing like possum's dust out there. Heard there was a bad wreck on the Raccoon River bridge." She strode around, spreading her abusive pessimism like fairy dust. I noticed that Polly turned away as soon as she saw her. She quickly slid back in her rocker and turned toward the wall, as if she were trying to blend into the scenery. Velmajean approached her in her pushy style.

"Well, look who is back here, our Princess Pinny. Now listen here, you ain't to be running off or stealing food. Dr. Steiner says you are gaining too much weight with all of your thieving."

Polly recoiled. Velmajean was like an ill-tempered rattlesnake. She belittled people and repeatedly nagged them. Nearly everything she did was abusive. Birdie told me that Velmajean had been raised in a tarpaper shack and had seen her share of bad men over the years.

"There are good souls and bad souls on this earth. And there are hollow souls whose feelings are only influenced by drugs and alcohol. Long ago, Velmajean hollowed out her soul to protect herself. She is like a shell from the sea, hard on the outside and dark and empty within. Don't expect regret or apologies from a hollow soul."

Thanksgiving came and went. Much to the relief of my sisters and me, my older brother Kevin came home from college for a few days. "Kevy," as he had once been affectionately known, was a poster child for parental commentary. He chewed audibly, slouched, and ate without utensils. He had grown his hair into a long wild pony tail. On good days, he was awake by 2:00 p.m. and his hair was braided. On bad days, his breakfast was dinner. He rambled on about Hare Krishna and Buddha. He spoke of the Buddhist respect for animals after Dad threatened the squirrels of America.

"I'll poison those damn squirrels if they keep messing with my birdfeeder. All my goldfinches are gone now!"

"In Buddhist tradition, killing of animals should always be avoided."

"Well, I don't think Señor Buddha had to contend with rodents like these."

Kevy did his best to stay calm and demonstrate good Karma. This whole dispute seemed unnecessary, but families just love to 'keep things going' sometimes. Who knows why?

"Animals may very well be reborn human beings. The spirit of your grandmother might reside in a squirrel or a bird."

Dad suddenly had one of his animated little spells. You could watch the blood pour into his face. He got louder, and his speech was accelerated. It was almost like a brief burst of mania in a generally flat-lined life.

"My grandmother is now a squirrel? I think you should lay off smoking the curry powders and the poppy seeds!"

"The goldfinches do not belong to you. You created artificial dependence by feeding them in the first place. You wanted your own little bird show and are annoyed that other animals want to eat, too?"

"We created artificial dependence by feeding you every day. Feel free to return to your rigorous schedule in your Eastern philosophy classes."

At that, Kevy smiled and asked Mom for another heaping helping of her self-created "gobbleroll," a holiday turkey pot pie topped with tube rolls. Kevy loved all of Mom's food, so he received her favor. He offered to play some relaxing guitar music after dessert. Colleen winked at me; we knew this was our ticket out. Mom could pretend that Kevy was George Harrison, Kevy could hope that his impromptu concert extended his eating binge, and Dad would soon be snoring in front of the television.

Colleen later tapped on my bedroom door. It was our time to take a walk! She never knocked loudly because we did not want to disturb the "family harmony." Our street stood on a hill above the Raccoon River. There was a well-worn path that we could access through a hole in our backyard fence. Knee high weeds led to a dark pine grove. We were forbidden from smoking at home, so we usually went to the woods to grab a couple. As an added bonus, Colleen had slipped two beers away from the garage fridge and stuffed them into her tie-dyed Grateful Dead bag. The snaps of the beer can tabs echoed through the woods. Colleen took an extra-long swig of beer and broke the ice.

"So, do you think that Kevy is still serenading his mommy with a guitar solo?"

We laughed explosively.

"Honestly, I think he would do anything for food. He would try to do a cartwheel for a sandwich if he knew what a cartwheel was!"

Our laughter was loud and a bit shivery in the November air.

"I am not sure what they do at college, but he seems to know less now than when he went away!"

Colleen stood up and paced around, continuing with her commentary.

"Remember when Mom would make him, 'Kevy- skettie' because he used to gag on everything? While the rest of us choked down that canned 'Salmon Delight,' he sat there every night until age sixteen with his cut-up spaghetti and mashed up meatball. Topped with that spray can cheese."

We laughed again!

I picked up where Colleen had left off. "The whole freezer in the garage was full of precut bags of 'Kevy-skettie'! Mom made them ahead of time because you just never knew when Kevy was going to hurl! Then Kevy would only drink milk through a straw. I was so mad one night. I sat down to a pork-chop dinner, and Mom suddenly flipped out because we were out of straws. My bike had a flat tire, so they made me walk down to Big Al's grocery store to buy him some damn straws. I was ravenous, and when I got back, everyone else had eaten anyway.

There sat 'King Kevy' waiting for his straw. For a while, Dad kept an old fishing bucket under the dining room table in case dinner didn't agree with Kevy because he never seemed to know enough to run off to the bathroom!"

"No!" Colleen shrieked.

"Yes, he did! And, remember the medication? He had to take some pills for mysterious allergies, but, of course, he would gag on those, too. There was pleading, begging, and bribery, but none of that worked. He would just gag and then we were out some more pills. So, Mom actually baked him his own pie whenever he needed to be medicated. I was so angry. King Kevy, with all of his allergies, ate his own chocolate cream pie. Because Mom didn't know exactly where the pills were located, we couldn't have any. She told us that we could have raisins! Turns out he had found the pills anyway and spit them out into his napkin!"

We quickly worked our way back up hill as our hands were freezing. Like teenaged bulls, our exhaled smoke preceded us. Colleen reminisced about the Grateful dead concert she had snuck off to in Rochester a couple of months previously.

"It was so awesome! Magnificent! Peace-loving people, dancing carefree and barefoot! Everyone in the same groove!"

She spun around with her signature hippie flair, her skirt rotating like an open umbrella.

CHAPTER FOUR

One day in early December, I arrived home from work in the late afternoon. The house smelled of singed butter, the phone was ringing loudly, and Dad was ladling out canned tomato soup. What resembled burned grilled-cheese sandwiches sat on a platter. I grabbed the screeching phone because I had no idea what was going on. On the other end of the line was my Mom's sister Lorna who said that it was urgent that she speak to my father. He spoke to her in hushed tones and utterances. Rita walked in quickly and asked if I had heard the latest. She said that Colleen hadn't come home last night. Mom was over at Aunt Lorna's for consolation. Dad announced that dinner was ready.

"We are having dinner while Colleen is missing?"

"No one has determined that Colleen is missing, young man. She didn't make curfew last night but was out with her boyfriend, so I have made a call to his parents. I am sure we will hear from them soon."

"When was she last seen?"

"She punched out at the restaurant at 9:30 last night."

"I am going to look for her!"

He was still carrying on as I left in fury.

"I work all week to put food on the table, and this is the gratitude…."

Despite the snow, I took my ten speed. My army trench coat was awkward on a bike, so I unbuttoned it. It looked a bit like a sail as it flew behind me. I stopped at the DiStefanos. Joey was retrieved by his Grandmother. He looked tense, weak, and pale.

"I talked to your father already and told him I didn't see Colleen last night. I was sick with a fever and still am. I know she was working last night until around nine. That is all I know. I am really sorry. Tell your Aunt Lorna to leave us alone. She has a few screws loose and is threatening us by phone."

I went to the Meat-n-Taters diner, the truck stop where Colleen worked. I walked in from the wet weather to the stink of old chili and fry grease. Lonely looking men listened to twangy country music while the matronly waitress, Miss Jeannie, tended to them. It was a sad-looking place, and I suddenly felt overwhelmingly sorry for Colleen, wherever she was. I asked Miss Jeannie if she had seen anyone talking with Colleen before she left.

"You don't think anyone here bothered your sister, do you? I would check on that boyfriend of hers. We run a clean establishment. Colleen is a free spirit, so who knows, she may have just run off. She complained to me quite a bit about how restrictive your parents are and how stifled she was. Sometimes, teenagers just run off when they see no other way out."

Amid the cold stares of the truckers, I left more confused than ever. So far, nobody seemed to have any clues or anything else to offer. I rode my bike, gravitating to the sidewalk because it was past dark. While pedaling away, I wept briefly but fiercely, my tears mixing with the wet snow. I had some kind of panic attack, an excited feeling amid a great deal of dread. I saw Colleen, dark haired and dancing in circles. She believed in witchcraft, spells, voodoo, and unicorns. She loved to wear long denim skirts and adorn herself with leather, amulets, and sea shells. She braided her long shiny hair with feathers and beads. She was a mid-70's version of a hippie, witchy woman who had threatened to run away with Gypsies. Her easy smile as a child had inverted in adolescence into a perpetual pout. As her quirky, Bohemian appearance changed like the seasons, my parents kept trying to rope her back in. Colleen's unbridled, unconventional beliefs clashed with the boring values that spewed out of my parents. My sister had said how much she had looked forward to getting out of town. After a couple of beers, which we cracked open by the river, she had told me about her strong desire to live in a big city. She said that while her mind raced with thoughts and ideas, much of the world seemed dead to her. She said that she and Joey spent most of their time together trying to outdo each other with ridiculous familial beliefs and traditions. She despised cliques and small minded, small town gossip. It was as if her stabs at self-expression were lost on a disinterested rural audience and parents who hid deep within the status quo of their neutral-toned, split-level space in dullsville.

Colleen had not come home! I suddenly remembered what I was doing. As I got closer to home, that sick, worried feeling returned. It occurred to me that I hadn't eaten anything. I rode to Donut Delight and ordered some gloppy, sloppy donuts. I washed them down with a cup of hot coffee. After my gluttonous respite, I rode home. The house was lit up and there were a few extra cars in the driveway. I tried to sneak in the garage door to find Rita, but the dreaded Aunt Lorna found me. Ah, now lonely Aunt Lorna had taken up roost in our home. Aunt Lorna seemed to have many one-time dates and just as many short-term jobs. Masterful at initial manipulation, Lorna spun comfortable little webs for everyone she knew. She was a crafty spider who entertained and engaged her guests. Quickly and predictably, things would always change. Lorna had a childlike need for attention and an insatiable appetite for medical maladies. She claimed allergies to shellfish, nuts, corn, berries, tomatoes, garlic, and onions. She had sensitivities to beans, milk, yogurt, and apple cider. Stews and gravies could cause her patented "sour stomach." Unexplained rashes and patches flared up all over her body, and she thought nothing of showing them off, no matter where they were located! She loved to talk about her physical conditions. She spared no details. She was routinely in excruciating pain. Her legs would go numb or her arms would tingle. She was the victim of spasms, palsies, and seizures. Her welcome in the emergency room was long worn out. She was a willing participant in any surgery. My mother, her devoted sister, was her nursemaid for most of her adult life. Lorna loved the phone. She frequently called doctors. She easily got jobs and quickly left them. Her physical conditions, each one more dramatic than the last one, always got in the way of gainful employment. If she felt that she wasn't getting enough attention, she threatened people with lawsuits or the police. She was usually quarreling with neighbors about everything from the length of their grass to the frequency of their visitors. Each winter, she was good for at least one fall on the ice. This was a given. She likely gained insurance payouts and won minor lawsuits due to her abilities as a diagnostic soliloquist. Mixing anatomical and disease-ridden terminology, she bored listeners and passersby. Her life was one long medical filibuster. She had a closet full of slings, canes, bandages, and even a wheelchair. Colleen and I laughed for hours at her soap opera-like "temporary blindness" and the time she broke the bone in her upper arm, "the humerus." As kids, of course, we thought she broke her "humorous." Colleen, in her brief stab at poetry, had written the following:

"Lorna, dorna, with a whiney old tone,
  fell and broke her funny bone
  and ever since her tragic tumble,
all she does nothing but gloom and grumble.'

Standing with hands on hips in the hallway, Lorna began her interrogation.

"Where have you been while your family is suffering so? I am having a terrible sciatica flare up, and now I have to take all this on, too!"

"I was out looking for my sister!"

Lorna wedged her girth in the hallway so that I could not pass by her.

"Your father has been on the phone all night. Leave the police work to the professionals. You don't know what you are doing. I am having blood drawn tomorrow, so one of you will have to step up and help your mother. My health is going downhill."

"I need to get by, please."

"Your mother has taken to her bed and is under a doctor's care. And you are out riding a bike through the snow like some sort of teenaged deputy? This whacky family will be the death of me yet!"

At that, I left, scurrying out through the garage door. I rapped on Rita's window, and she let me in through her room.

Rita looked at me with concern. "I don't know where she is!"

"Come with me in the morning, Rita. We will look ourselves—we have to."

"I won't know where to begin."

"Get up early and come with me. We need to get the hell out of here. We have to look for her."

Amid a light angelic snowfall, Rita and I snuck out of the house at daybreak. As soon as we were out of view, we lit up some cigs and planned out a route. We exhaled deeply, our toxic smoke drifting through the fluffy flakes.

"We need to look by the river," I said.

"How was she supposed to get home after work?"

"We have to figure that out. Dad told me that she was with Joey, but Joey told me that he was sick."

"He was sick. Colleen told me that he was absent when I saw her in the cafeteria at school. She said that he had a fever."

"Then wouldn't she have asked Dad for a ride? I'll go back to the diner later to see if they remember how she left."

Rita and I spontaneously developed our own investigation system. We called it 20/60. We walked twenty paces together, turned in opposite directions, and scanned the area for at least one minute. We became acutely aware of the misery of the Raccoon River. We hit all of the secret little party spots. We saw beer bottles, band aids, and wads of toilet paper. We found an appliance-dumping graveyard, with a rusty stove and a refrigerator door. We saw broken glass, garbage, and a damp book from the school library last checked out to a Robbie Green. We smelled spilled beer and the resulting stale urine. The taller the trees were, the stronger the earthen mushroomy odor. We found no trace of Colleen. We found nothing at all.

I am dreaming that we are kids riding ponies at the county fair. The ponies lazily limp around in a circle as if in a trance. Occasionally, they nod their heads and shake off the flies. Pounding the sawdust, they seem bored and disheartened. Colleen's pony seems to be bothered by a bee. The pony bucks and stomps around and my sister looks truly frightened. A skinny carnie man in a black tee shirt gives the pony a whack, which makes the situation worse. None of the ponies are moving. We are all asked to dismount. Colleen looks afraid and leaps off suddenly.

I woke with my heart ablaze, having no idea what time it was. It was 4:30 a.m. I suddenly recalled that I had to work at 7:00. I had forgotten about work despite being reminded last night at dinner that "life goes on and there comes a point when your old routine is your salvation."

I couldn't go back to sleep, so decided to walk to work. While it would take a good hour to get up there, I felt as though I could keep searching along the way. I left Rita a note because I couldn't remember if she knew I was working. Off I went into the frigid morning. I looked everywhere along the way, adjusting 20/60 for one. I saw trees that I had never seen. A beautiful doe ran across Asylum Road. I heard a murder of crows cackling and screeching, their shattering chatter piercing the dawn. I saw an empty car off the road with a flat tire. I went past the entrance to the Black Bear campground. The huge bear sculpture was peeling and shabby. The owner of the next house seemed a little behind on the holidays. There was a plastic skeleton dangling from a flagpole and a long-forgotten display of pumpkins, now rotting and deflated. I found no trace of Colleen. I found nothing at all.

I went into the ward at Smokey Hollow. Without any breezy ventilation, the ward was hot and had a stale odor. The excessive heat boiled an odd stench into the air. The janitor in the ward smelled of farm work himself, so it all tended to blend together.

Birdie greeted me with concern. Some of her friends had heard on the scanner that my sister was a possible victim of a crime. I hadn't even been thinking of that possibility. Her words startled me. In a small town, the scanner gets a lot of use. It is the newspaper and the rumor mill. Some live vicariously through the scanner. There are gruesome details available for all to hear—people burned alive, decapitated, fished out of rivers, and long since gone, whereabouts unknown.

The rocker was empty and still.

"Where is Polly today?"

"According to her ward, she is in the infirmary under the care of Nurse Giles and Superintendent Steiner. They said she may be there a few days for testing."

Suddenly, I had a chill. I shook and shivered. Dad had said that these were likely seizures as well. The day at work was fairly mundane and miserable. I missed Polly's smile and seemed paralyzed by my sister's predicament. Three more days passed. And three dark, cold nights went by. Rita and I searched when we could and some friends joined us. Birdie brought a psychic to look near the river. Colleen hated the cold, so I started to believe that she had taken a Greyhound bus to Florida or California. I was confident that she would call soon or send a tropical postcard. I envisioned that she already had a job, perhaps in a warm restaurant. Arriving home from work one day, I saw a police car in the driveway. I thought it was likely the usual update without any real news. But this day was different. Rita saw me coming up the walk and dashed out into the cold.

"They found her purse and locket down near Sandstone Creek."

"Grab your coat and we'll go."

We ran a bit to escape the radius of our home. We went to Sandstone Creek. Rita and I saw a police car there and a couple of officers looking through the weeds. While it was frightening watching them search, it was that much worse not knowing where she was. I had imaginary conversations with my sister, and this was likely the worst possible scenario. If Colleen had been able to decide her own fate, I was quite certain that she would have preferred a mystery. She would have hated someone finding her muddy locket and her frozen purse. Rumors would start. Scanners would crackle. Her life would forever be a town legend, with scraps of truth attached to a bulletin board of empty dreams. Where was she? Was it foul play? Had she ditched her things and run off? Had she provided a diversionary trail? When would this nightmare end? Would it ever end?

Polly came back to the ward a few days later. She grinned ear to ear when she saw me. I had begun to play music for her while she rocked. I called it, "rocking rock." She loved the music of the Jackson Five in particular, so I always had a cassette handy to liven things up. Vina caught the rhythm on occasion as well and drew it into her stereotypic spinning routines. We had to be cautious about our music, and it all had to cease by afternoon, lest Velmajean find out that we were trying to have some fun. I asked Birdie about Christmas, wondering if there was any sort of party or gift exchange for the residents.

"Superintendent Steiner reminds us every year that the state doesn't add any special reimbursement during the month of December. They have a nice meal on Christmas. He says that we can't have a big holiday celebration because some of the residents are not Christian and it would only remind them that their families had abandoned them."

"Well, he has an answer for everything."

"Well, he runs the place."

"Well, I have never even seen him."

I called grizzled Uncle Willie and asked if I could go up and see him. Willie was Dad's half-brother, a description used by my mother when she needed to put intentional distance between them. Willie was a favorite of mine, but he was a man of the hills nonetheless. He lived in a mobile home up off of Blackberry Run. He dabbled in taxidermy and whiskey, and played the fiddle in a band known as The Nitpickers. He always had a few critters undergoing reconstruction. When I was a kid, he had a pet crow named Poe, and I loved playing with him. Poe would bring me shiny bits that Willie had strewn about the property to keep the bird occupied. Eventually, Poe went to meet his maker. Uncle Willie decided that his pet crow would be a nice taxidermy project, so he was currently on the wall between a deer head and an old muskrat. To say that Willie was an odd bird was an understatement. He made macaroni and cheese every Sunday and ate it for the next four nights straight. He took his other three dinners down at the Hitching Post Tavern because the Nitpickers were usually on the stage later in the evening. Well, it wasn't really a stage; it was more like a raised corner. It was set back far enough to keep the wobbly, drunken softball players from stumbling over the drum set. Mom had told me that Uncle Willie had been married once, but his wife had run off with a biker. It seemed that since then he had lost interest in most people and preferred skinning dead animals to human relationships. Most of his taxidermy work was done in his shed, a smelly, dimly lit out building that always looked to be on the verge of collapse. Glass eyes, body forms, bleach, and tanning oils gave the shed a Halloween feeling all year round. Perhaps because Uncle Willie was so adept at bringing dead animals back to life through taxidermy, so too was he able to nurse wounded animals back to health. While he never had a "critter doctor" sign out front, he was known far and wide for his extraordinary touch at animal rehabilitation. In a small town, everyone knows who has a skill through word of mouth. The Yellow Pages aren't needed. Uncle Willie had his own group of core pets. At any given time, he had three or four dogs. The number of cats was never exact because their headquarters were in the barn. Just as often as one of them ran off or died caught up on barbed wire in the woods, a new litter would be suckling somewhere in the hay. His, "KITTENS 4 SALE" sign stood year-round at the road. Uncle Willie had a pair of goats that we named "Baby Jane" and "Norman Bates." Their adorable progeny graced many farms throughout the area. Baby Jane was fickle about being milked. As often as she was cooperative, she would kick and stomp like a wild boar. Our uncle had a permanent possum named Jethro. His mother had been smashed along the roadside, and Jethro never developed enough skills to be on his own. Heck, he didn't even know how to play possum. We kids thought that Willie adored Jethro and never taught him the survival skills because he didn't want him to leave. Often, we snuck up to Willie's menagerie. Mom never went there; she called it "a smelly, chicken wire zoo." Dad referred to it as "the roadkill ranch on the hill."

He had a large turkey vulture that was blessed with one and a half wings. The poor thing would flap about repeatedly to try and become airborne. Colleen and I had named her "Waddle Mae" due to her wild gait. Waddle Mae was the perfect complement to a taxidermy shed. After Willie extracted the skin and fur or feathers, the pink-headed bird would bat clean up and consume the leftovers. She picked clean every carcass efficiently and consumed all varieties of carrion and offal. Willie referred to her as his "waddling graveyard."

One of the stars of Willie's critter show was a clumsy fawn named "Rudolph." The little buck had some unfortunate snout issues, causing his nose to appear swollen and reddish. Rudy was just semi-tame so would drop in when he wanted. Uncle Willie put out a salt lick and some carrots in December so the young buck could be seen before the holidays. Townsfolk and hill people came to get a gander at the "red nosed deer." As a kid of seven or so, I asked about Rudy frequently; I never saw him again after that winter. My uncle told me that he had been chosen for Santa's team and went to the North Pole. A few years later, my father told me that the deer had been struck and killed by "a pickup full of redneck friends of your uncle." "Hootie" was his barn owl who had arrived with a broken wing. While the wing mended, Hootie seemed emotionally unable to leave. Perhaps it was the raw hamburger that we served her each day. She was loud and had a ghostly, heart-shaped face. She became heavy set and lost an eye in some kind of wild, territorial dispute with Poe. My favorite of the rare animals was

"Miss Kitty," a gorgeous red fox who had lost one of her paws in a trap. She had a pungent den on the edge of the property. She was left some scraps each day because she was unable to hunt efficiently with her hobbling gate. On rare occasions, the shy fox would come out for food while I waited there. Skittish and suspicious, she dragged her meal backward into her burrow amid some tree roots. If the cats had gone mousing, I would take the dazed critters to Miss Kitty, who seemed especially pleased if they were still living. She also seemed quite happy if Willie sent her a pigeon or a hen that had keeled over. One day, I noticed another, younger looking fox taking her food back to the den.

"Uncle Willie, there is a new fox stealing Miss Kitty's food!"

"Not to worry about it. That is one of her kits come back to feed her."

"Where is Miss Kitty then?"

"She is in her tunnel there by the tree. It is likely she can't walk no more."

"Can't we do something to help her?"

"Comes a time when you can't do no more. Her youngin is here to help her. Foxes are like that. Kitty is going on five years old. She ain't got much time left."

With that, I walked away and cried, briefly. I wasn't sure about this animal business because I hated it when they went away. When Kitty died, her little one reverently buried her. She kicked dirt back into the den for a few hours, carefully filling in the hole. I helped her by placing a large rock there. Willie gave me some paint, and I wrote on the rock in a childish script:

'Here lies Miss Kitty. Sweet friend from the Wild. Devoted to her kits.'

I updated Willie on my parents' present situation.

"My parents are losing it. The house is a mess. Mom is doped up, and Dad is talking to the TV! He asks Aunt Bea for advice and spends way too much time watching *Perry Mason* and *The Twilight Zone*."

"Your Mama is doped up because my brother is a dope. Always

has been."

"We don't know what to do."

"Did they find out anything more about Colleen?"

"No, nothing. No one knows where she is."

"Well, someone in that town saw something. They ain't talking is all."

"Can you talk to my Dad?"

"Nope, never could. I will see what I can find out about your sister. I'll ask around. I called your house a few times, but I see they have lazy Lorna at the reception desk. I hung up on her. She squawks on more than a chicken that is lined up to have its throat cut."

Uncle Willie reached up, pulled Poe down off the wall, and handed the crow to me. He was dusty and much lighter in his new form, but he was beautiful nonetheless with his charcoal sheen. No matter what happened, Willie always made me feel better in a way that no one else could. He stood at a necessary, generous distance from his family but always treated me with respect.

CHAPTER FIVE

Just before Christmas, Polly was rocking out to the Jackson Five. Suddenly, the door opened with a shocking thud. The noise of the door drowned out my fumbling with the cassette, so the fact that we were trying to enjoy ourselves was not discovered. Musty strode in with his key ring. A short, ugly man who wore a bow tie followed. His face was pinched in a pained expression reflecting either chronic constipation or gas withheld. Musty, as if he were making a pronouncement from the king, indicated that Superintendent Steiner had an important message about a new charge being brought to the ward.

"The specimen is an unfortunate victim of anencephaly. The cranium is absent of a brain, and the back of the skull is open. We will cover it with a sock. There is no activity beyond brainstem functioning. He will only live a few days or perhaps a week. His parents were too distraught to give him a name; therefore, we will refer to him as Baby X."

With that pronouncement, the two creeps left.

I turned to Birdie and said, "I'd like to cover their heads with socks."

She winked at me.

A nurse from the infirmary marched in later that day carrying a box. It was a shoe box to be more precise. She presented the box to Birdie, and we read the instructions that were taped on the side over a picture of work boots.

"Baby X. ANENCEPHALIC. Brainstem functioning only. Groundbreaking research to be conducted by Elbert Steiner, M.D. DO NOT RESUSCITATE.

Birdie looked at me, possible anticipating commentary.

"Well, I guess Steiner should add 'psychic' to his resume as he seems to know that he will be doing 'groundbreaking research' before any of it actually happens!"

Birdie and I peered into the shoe box. Baby X, as he was known, lay still, his skin a grayish color. He was diapered and his blanket, if you will, was another diaper. Crowned with a cut-off tube sock, he had an appearance of contentment in his expression. His breathing became a focal point because we were told that it would suddenly end.

Polly came back the next day and immediately went to Baby X's box, as if she had seen him before. She took him to the rocking chair and started her lurching movements, forward and back, forward and back. At one point, she rocked so hard that Baby X began to slide out of his little box. I retrieved him and put my hand on Polly's shoulder to slow her down a bit. She winced. I asked if she was hurt, and she pulled up her sleeve. I noticed several vaccination scars, bruising, and recent needle marks. I brought this to Birdie's attention, and she reminded me that Polly had been in the infirmary recently. We checked in on Baby X. No change. Later a nurse came down with a wheelchair. Polly and Baby X were being summoned for testing. Polly became slightly agitated when she saw the nurse. When I turned Baby X over to the nurse, Polly got into the chair and complied. I wasn't clear on what all this testing was but had learned from Dan not to poke a snake with a stick.

My brother Kevy called. He was unable to deal with Colleen's situation in the midst of the parental paralysis. He asked if I would be able to visit him at the State University to talk about everything that was going on. He said that an old friend of the family, Rick LaChance was heading that way and I could ride along with him. I jumped at the chance. I had two days off and needed a change. While it was easier for everyone to have Kevy stay at school, I wanted his advice. We went to the Rathskeller, a dim basement bar on campus. While speaking with Kevy, I realized that I had never really had a conversation with him that wasn't hijacked or interrupted. I barely knew him. He had always been a little odd and eccentric. He kept to himself and hid in his lair above the garage. His room had only been partially finished. Dad had repeatedly claimed that he had new plans for finishing the room, but in truth, it was never done. Kevy hung posters over spots where dry-wall was never installed. He draped Christmas lights into a corner because the overhead light had never been added. The room weirded me out, so I rarely went near it.

"Kevy, Mom and Dad are losing it. Lorna is sharing all kinds of new pills with Mom, and Dad is talking to Aunt Bea and Della Street!"

"We need to get Lorna out of there. She must be due for crutches again soon. I'll call Mom and tell her. She usually listens to me."

"Uncle Willie is trying to get more information about Colleen. He won't talk to Dad, but he is trying to help as best he can."

"When I talk to Mom, I will ask her how Dad is. Lorna is likely commanding all of the attention, but she will soon get tired. Lorna despised Colleen because she was on to her fake sickness gigs. Remember the hysterical blindness caused by exposure to a solar eclipse? I can still hear her whining and tapping her cane."

"Kevy, I can't pass by Colleen's room. I can't look at her things. I spend as much time as I can away from home. Please talk to Mom. They are falling apart."

The beer did the rest of the talking. Kevy did his best to make me feel comfortable. He went so far as to get some stained couch cushions from the student lounge and borrowed a slippery sleeping bag. Every time the sleeping bag slid, the cushions would separate, causing some part of my body to sag to the floor.

The next day, Kevy and I went to the dining hall for some breakfast. My ride back with Rick was a couple of hours away, but Kevy had a class. He didn't seem to know which class it was, so I had the impression that he was trying to put on a good show for me. He thought that I might want to see the college library, so he dropped me off there. I drifted from area to area and found a section with books about diseases and medical conditions. I paged through books containing grainy photographs of people who had congenital anomalies and rare disorders. I saw photos of people who had progeria, which causes premature aging. I learned about cretinism and gigantism. I saw babies born with phocomelia, in which limbs were often absent, with hands and feet attached directly to the torso. Ironically, their mothers may have been given the drug thalidomide to combat the morning sickness associated with pregnancy. I was fascinated by a syndrome known as "Cri-du-Chat," in which the baby cries like a cat. I read about anencephaly, and what we had been told about Baby X seemed fairly accurate. He might live a few days or weeks. I paged through the rest of the book and at last found a photo of someone who looked exactly like Polly. He could have been her twin. According to the book, this gentleman had microcephaly, which caused changes to the shape of his skull. I quickly made a photocopy of the page because I realized that I needed to get uptown to meet Rick.

The next day, I returned to work. I checked on Baby X. He looked bluish, but I could see that he was breathing. He was still covered with a fine layer of hair. Birdie called it goose down, but I could never remember the real name for it. She had brought in a little afghan for him, and I wrapped him in it after checking on him. We were secretive with his little blanket because we were under orders to pretend that we didn't care about him. The nurse who would come to fetch him was usually loud and disruptive anyway, so that was our signal to hide the afghan. Because Polly was so fond of milkweed, we had named the baby after her favorite plant. Birdie and I could not bring ourselves to refer to him as Baby X any longer. While we had accepted that he would die, we wanted him to be comfortable within the time that he had with us. I gave him some water though a medicine dropper. I tried to curl his hand around my fingers, but his arm fell limp into the box. I had hoped his eyes would open or he would fuss somehow, but he did neither.

Polly arrived, and she took to Milkie like his mother. She started rocking him as soon as she had taken her boots off. The chair was beginning to leave ruts in the floor in a circular pattern. When Polly got the chair fired up, she would spin in circles and smile at those with whom she made eye contact. She seemed so happy in her chair.

Rita and I shared custody of the family cars, but one had been neglected and she was unable to pick me up after work. I decided to walk and get some more 20/60 time in. I noticed activity at the house next to Black Bear campground where I had seen the outdated Halloween display. There was a dark station wagon labeled "County Coroner" and a police car in the driveway. I could see a black bag, likely containing a body, through the back window. A sick feeling came over me, and I felt disappointed in myself. I had stopped at this house when I was first looking for Colleen. I had noticed the old decorations. Had I looked further, I would have seen the soggy, overflowing newspapers and the snow-packed front steps. One of the downspouts had separated from the gutters and dangled at the side of the house. I should have seen these things the first time. As I walked on, I developed a sinister jealousy of the family of the deceased. While their loved one may have been dead for weeks, at least they had a body. They could help write a proper obituary. Even if no one had seen the dead person for months, they would be able to tidy it all up in the local newspaper. A cranky old hermit can become a "caring grandfather." A hoarder, rotting away amid garbage and magazines can become a "loving servant of our Lord, Jesus." The family could throw a wake, or, for convenience, hold a graveside service. The house could be cleaned up and long-lost relatives could pick through everything, like chickens in corn feed. In ignorance, they would make fun of older items and likely throw valuable things away. But the family had a body. The house would be sold. There would be grousing about fair shares. Some would threaten to sue each other or storm off never to speak to their kin folk again.

With my sister, we had nothing. The only evidence found had led to more unanswered questions. Her purse contained her license and ten dollars. It was difficult to believe that these things were recovered. Yet the wad of cash she kept in her sweater drawer was missing. Only Rita and I knew that it was gone. Did she leave us? Did she get so sick of my parents that she ran off? Did she have a fight with Joey? Did a trucker pick her up and kidnap her? It was so awful. It was excruciating. One day everything had changed. I had started to make up possible scenarios in my head. In every one of them, Colleen was alive and well. This was the best that I could do for her.

Out of complete and utter morbid curiosity, I phone Donnie Wayne Briggs to find out more about the occupant of the house. Predictably, he knew all the details. His father, the "commander," was first on the scene. The grandson of the deceased said that he hadn't answered the phone in weeks. Donnie Wayne told me that Alvin Phelps had dropped dead at breakfast and went face first into a bowl of cereal. There he sat for several weeks. When the rescue squad tried to loosen up the rigor enough to tip him into a stretcher, the bowl went with him. The attendants couldn't bring themselves to try and separate it, so he went into the bag with a bowl on his face. His poor poodle had taken to the basement during the ordeal and was discovered belly-up next to the furnace.

My family was stuck in a purgatory of doubts and rumors. We were trying to tread water in quicksand. There were "no new leads," and Colleen was still gone. My conscious mind kept her alive. She would write me soon and tell me about sunny Florida. Maybe she just needed some time away. Or she would give us a call and we would excitedly pass the phone back and forth to each other.

I can only see her in dreams. *We are kids, playing kickball with the neighbors. Colleen runs back to the woods to find the ball. The game is delayed while Colleen is searching through the prickly brambles. Where is she? Rita is annoyed and goes up into the woods to find her. Suddenly,*

Colleen dashes out from behind a tree and screams like a banshee. Rita screams back. The dream ends.

In another, *Colleen is the star in the Junior Ponytail Parade on Main Street. Sequined and strutting in white cowgirl boots, she charms the crowd with her coy smile and her precise command of the baton. She twirls herself around while she dramatically tosses her baton as high as the street lights. Her boots click on the pavement. Her movements accelerate as the crowd applauds wildly. With that, she is gone. The parade ends in silent, slow motion.*

In one of my favorite dreams, *We are fishing at the river with Uncle Willie. He has an angry, unruly raccoon on a leash. He stakes the vermin to a tree, and we don't go near it. We fish away, on the lazy, humid afternoon. Uncle Willie tells tales of his mother, our Grandpa's third wife.*

"Tell us about her pipe."

"Well, Colleen, she had herself a handmade, corn cob pipe. Mama didn't have no teeth, but she sure loved her tobacco. One day, she dragged too hard on the thing and sucked it clear in and started to choke. The smoke was right under her eyes, so she teared up. Her eyes bugged clear out of her head. Her sister Ivetta had to slap her a couple of good ones to shake the dang pipe loose."

Laughter fills the stinky river air.

"Your Grandpa thought Mama wasn't laundering things proper. He took after her, sayin' that his pillow case smelled bad. He wouldn't let it go. Next day, Mama washed it real good. Then she hung it out of the line, with a dead fish dangling inside it on a clothes pin."

We laugh again. With that, Colleen is gone. The dream ends quietly.

At Smokey Hollow, Polly had become increasingly possessive of Milkie. She tapped him, perhaps expecting him to do more than he did. I had begun to tell her that the baby was sick. Polly rocked on, ignoring me. Polly was wearing the standard-issue institutional frock, and I noticed abundant coarse hair on her legs. Birdie said that she would mention it to her ward staff when they came to fetch her in the afternoon.

CHAPTER SIX

Christmas was a sad time. Colleen was still gone. Dad watched several Christmas specials and wept copiously. Mom quickly put out a few Christmas displays and then took to her bed. Colleen's favorite was a little doll-faced collection of Rudolphs, in honor of Uncle Willie's fawn. Each day, she mischievously moved them around the house. You might find a reindeer in your lunch bag or one sitting on top of the toilet tank. She would put them in cars, hanging from the rear-view mirror. Red-nosed friends would be seen crawling up walls or dangling from the shower-curtain rod. On Christmas morning, you might find one stuck to your face or pillow. They smelled strongly of plastic, and the colors were fading. Some had more of a dull pink nose.

Lorna apparently didn't like the way Mom had positioned the nativity display near the tree. As our aunt often did, she impulsively started rearranging things. In her haste, she hip-checked the tree, and it spilled over. Ornaments shattered and lights were broken. The tree stand spewed water across the hardwood floor. Globs of foil tinsel coagulated in the sticky pine needle mess. Of course, Lorna pretended to fall at the same time. She promptly blamed the fall on our dog, Jelly Beans. That was it! Without thinking, I quickly called the rescue squad. I had no idea what a beautiful decision this was! Commander Briggs was first to arrive on the scene. Long familiar with Lorna's phony calls, he yawned and left the incident to two inexperienced volunteers. Lorna craved paramedics and sirens. X-rays were ice cream to her. She was a victim again at last! All was well! I called her friend from the church so they could start a bedside vigil.

Rita and I worked together to pull off a Christmas Eve meal. We made a pasta casserole, complete with garlic and oregano. Dad had freshly showered and may have splashed some cologne here or there. Mom was still retaining her "laid up wear" with a stained bathrobe, but she did manage to smile a few times. I challenged the family to move the plastic reindeer around as Colleen would have wanted. Dad escorted Mom back to bed. While Rita and I were cleaning up, he came back and told us that Lorna was not coming back. He would deliver her overnight bag to the hospital and tell her there that we no longer needed her to stay at the house. Christmas had obviously come early!

On Christmas morning, there were no formal gifts. Rita made coffee and hot chocolate. She found some canned fruit, and I managed to prepare some toast. The fridge had gone sour, so there wasn't much else to eat. We somehow inspired our parents to go to church. While they were gone, Rita and I cleaned up the kitchen, with priority given to obvious mold and overdue expiration dates. Dejected, I went to the church hall before the services were ending because I had remembered that they had food available on holidays. The ladies from the church put leftovers from the Luncheon for the Homeless and Unfortunate into tinfoil containers. I got some ham and potatoes. It was terribly humiliating, especially knowing that my parents were upstairs at the same time. I managed to sneak away, and they never even asked where the food came from. I cleaned up Dad's TV tray and generously sprayed Lysol throughout the house.

In the morning, I fried some leftover ham before leaving for work. As I pulled out my chair in the kitchen, one of the plastic reindeer tumbled to the floor. It held a small piece of Christmas wrapping paper. In Mom's cursive was written, 'Thank you and Merry Christmas!'

When I got to work, Milkie and his boot resort were gone. I found Birdie, who quickly reassured me that he was at the infirmary.

"Oh, Steiner had some holiday inspiration for more groundbreaking research?"

Birdie smiled at me.

I tended to the other children with some morning hygiene. After everyone was freshened up, we played our own version of musical chairs. Gary was wheeled around at a high rate of speed and parked in front of the chair he was claiming. He loved going quickly and laughed until he cried. Vina stayed on the sidelines but I caught her watching us with curiosity. Polly arrived and seemed somewhat agitated. With Milkie gone, she didn't know quite what to do. I encouraged her to join the game, but she seemed disappointed when we kept turning the music off. She couldn't rock if we weren't going to provide the rhythm. In the end, we left the music on so she would calm down.

As we were feeding the kids at lunch, Birdie asked if I would like to visit her friend Virgil Fields. She told me that Virgil was a seer who spent his summers at Lily Dale in nearby Chautauqua County. In truth, I guess Virgil was a medium who was somehow able to retrieve messages from beyond. Lily Dale was a fascinating place in the warm months. Unhappy people flocked there, hoping that someone would predict that their fortunes would change. Suddenly, their dream job would appear! Miraculously, the person of their loving fantasies waited for them! And their dream boat would be rich to boot! More desperate were those people who came to speak to the departed. The grieving survivors so often repeated their unanswered questions.

"Did you know you were sick?"

"Why did you leave me so young?"

Or they try to rewrite history.

"If I had called the ambulance sooner, you would still be here."

"We should have gone to a different hospital."

Death, so personal to those who suffer, is still shrouded in mystery. We can't understand the culling of the herd or the trimming of the flock. We kill animals for pleasure and sustenance, but we can't understand why people die. I told Birdie that I would go, but I was reluctant nonetheless. I had never believed that Colleen was dead, but I understood that Virgil might offer another perspective. Perhaps he would suggest something we had overlooked. It was worth a shot.

Birdie came by in her pick up on a snowy evening, just before the New Year. The lake effect snow machine had set up, and there were a couple of feet already. Mercifully, Virgil didn't live far from town. We stomped off our boots in his garage and left them there before we entered his tiny abode. The little cottage smelled of incense or cloves. Virgil was a wisp of a man, short and frail. He walked with a pronounced limp. Surprisingly, his voice was larger than life. His well-chosen words filled the air. He had impeccable manners and thoughtful eyes. With tongue in cheek, he asked if I wanted the crystal ball or the tea leaves. I laughed but said that if he had a crystal ball, I would love to see it. There was clinking in the next room as he set up shop. Birdie, with her overwhelmingly reassuring demeanor, sat quietly. Virgil politely asked me to join him in a small dining room. A crystal ball sat in the center of the table. Strategically placed candles threw their light toward the crystal, as the flames flickered inside it. Ah, Colleen would love it here!

"Describe your sister to me."

"She is beautiful. She has long black hair and big cow eyes. She walks to the beat of a different drummer. She hates living here in town. She slings hash at the truck stop. My parents never really knew what to do with her. She believes in spirits, ghosts, and reincarnation. She is rebellious."

"Tell me where you think she is."

"She is probably in Florida or California. She is here, in my mind. I guess I don't really know where she is. This is where you come in."

"Do you accept that she will always be with you?"

"I accept."

Virgil closed his eyes and drifted into some sort of altered state. Colleen would have loved this scene, and I truly wished she were here to see it.

"There is a woman in town who knows more. Colleen met with her."

"Who? Who is it?"

"There is no way to know who it is right now. Colleen met with her and they spoke."

What else is there?"

"Nothing more. Nothing more tonight."

We left in the blinding snow. I could tell Birdie was getting anxious, so I told her to let me off a few streets away from home. I ran through tire tracks because nothing else had been shoveled.

The next day, a tense looking Joey DiStefano stood on our front porch. He was delivering a tray of holiday cookies from his family. Several of them watched tenuously from the car. I was getting used to morbidly nervous glances. Our family was suffering, yet people had begun to say less and stare more. We were unintentionally damaged goods. The possibility that Colleen had run off or been murdered was too much for us to bear. Yet our grief was somehow unbearable to others. Even the church people came less and less. There was no cookie tray from Reverend Hinckley. Not even a Christmas card.

I took Joey out through the garage.

"I heard that there is a woman in town who knows more about Colleen."

"I know there was the waitress up at the truck stop. Sandy Lynn Sawyer told my sister Denise that she waited on Colleen and Miss Curran, the guidance counselor, at Donut Delight. They were having coffee and talking about colleges. Sandy Lynn thought it was a little odd for them to be meeting at night."

"Thanks, Joey. I will follow up. If anyone remembers anything else, please let me know."

"I will. I feel so bad about all of this."

Energized by the shred of new information, I walked out to the long DiStefano station wagon. Grandpa, in broken English, warned me that anything wrapped in foil was soaked in rum. The cookie tray called to me as soon as I got inside. There were little squares with dates and nuts. There were light meringues and little tarts filled with pumpkin or fruit. Biscotti came in many varieties, begging to be plopped into a tall glass of milk. Amid the foiled rum balls were all kinds of other cookies that smelled of almonds, vanilla, and butter. I dove in, head first. Rum balls were first on the agenda.

I called the police about Colleen's meeting with Miss Curran. Rather than tipping her off myself, I had learned to take the investigative high road. I thought the whole thing sounded odd because Colleen had complained about Miss Curran and never seemed to like her. "Curious Curran," as she was known on the street, was not too popular for her outstanding guidance or life-changing advice. Instead, her daily sights seemed set on happy hour. She had a fine reputation for emptying pitchers and filling ash trays. She wisely walked to the bar, but trips home were known to be wobbly. She would stop and rest on porches without permission. Colleen told me that she once passed out in the hedges of a neighbor. She was so far gone, a rogue, unleashed dog started sniffing around her face. Grass stained, she arose and limped away. Her hair was stuck on one side of her face and her glasses were bent. She went home, spritzed herself up, and went to school to inspire the next generation.

Miss Curran spent so much time at Tipsie's Tavern that she had a special seat cushion on her bar stool and a cardigan sweater that hung on the back. She had memorized the entire jukebox and was known to sing way too loudly as the hours became "happier." She was constantly looking for foosball players. When she failed to find them, she slobbered up the pin ball machines, spilling beer and forgetting about ashy cigarettes. She was an awful darts player and had once "accidentally" thrown one at the bartender. She was bounced out on her ear that night but soon returned because the tavern, quite frankly, needed her money. As she loosened up, her chatter became incessant and her speech nearly incoherent. As drunks sometimes do, she became more emphatic and dramatic as the nights wore on. Most of the people she spoke at had utterly no interest in what she was saying. But she forcibly held them captive, so she thought, in her sloppy soliloquies. As she came out of her shell, most people wished that she had crawled back in.

I found Rita and updated her.

"Colleen was with Miss Curran at Donut Delight. Denise DiStefano heard that from someone who works there."

"What? She couldn't stand Curran."

"I called it in to the police. I can't take much more of this. She has been gone a month now, and we have nothing. I think about her all the time. I am really worried."

"Tell the police we want to meet with them. We need some answers. Every day that goes by is lost time."

"I will." I had stopped by Tipsies a few nights in a row but kept missing Miss Curran. I hadn't known the time of her precise arrival, but one evening I had better luck. There she sat in her dark little corner. The jukebox blared the blazing guitar of Lindsey Buckingham in Fleetwood Mac's "The Chain." Curran was loudly blathering to the bartender, complaining about one of the teachers at school.

"She struts around like she runs the world on her foolish high heels. She'll find out soon enough that nobody likes her. Nobody!"

As soon as she saw me approach her, she ordered another glass from the bartender. She looked genuinely disappointed when I declined. I told her that I had heard that she was seen with Colleen that night, and I wanted to know why that was.

"Your sister was looking at colleges. She desperately wanted to get out of this town. She couldn't stand living here anymore."

"Why were you meeting her at night?"

"We had scheduled meetings at school, but she kept missing them. Colleen skipped school a lot. She always said that her family didn't know her very well. I guess that was true, too."

With that, Curran gave a haughty little smirk.

"Well, if you know so much about her, where the hell is she?"

Loudly, she announced, "Step away from me or I will call the police. You have no right to question me like you are some kind of detective."

Again, I was furious!

"I am not going to leave anyone alone until I find my sister! Anyone!"

I stormed away. She started mouthing off drunken gibberish as I left, but I successfully ignored her and left her in her lonely corner. The door to Tipsies slammed behind me. I walked around town for a while. I had come to the conclusion that Colleen may have left town. That was the only common thread in the story at this point. She wasn't happy in school, she hated her stupid job, and her family didn't understand her. I was rapidly starting to envy her if she had run off. I felt as though I could have easily been right behind her. If I had known where she was, I would have hopped on the next Greyhound to be reunited.

That night, I drifted off into a dream. *The town is celebrating Founding Father's Day. There are long-winded speeches in the town square honoring the legacies of one Jedediah Weber and some other guy who had a beard. Colleen and I are pre-teens and waiting for the start of the Founder's Parade. The adults in front are dressed in burlap Civil War–looking clothes and are sweating profusely in the hot summer sun. A few of the men are on horseback. Our banana bikes are decked out in patriotic crepe paper streamers, woven through the spokes and dangling from the handle grips. Bored by the windbaggery, we begin to take note of those around us. Colleen nods toward the Lumpkin clan, perfectly postured on their family tandem bicycles. Ordinarily, this section of the parade is full of kids, but the Lumpkin parents, Larry and Faith, are positioned at the front of each of the double bikes. Their dutiful progeny, Simon and Magdalena, are tethered to the back seats with red and blue straps. Rumor has it that Simon sometimes quivers and quakes on the tandem, causing instability and the risk of a spillover. The Lumpkins are covered in stars and stripes like human flags. They wait motionless, like a family of birds, for the signal to start pedaling. Mercifully, the mayor's lecture is cut short by intense feedback from the speaker system. We begin our slow ride down Main Street. Sparse crowds wave from their portable lawn chairs. We spy Aunt Lorna, all decked out for the celebrations with a fresh limp and a new cane. Simon Lumpkin adds a piercing shriek as his father briskly turns the bike to avoid careening through horse dung. Colleen winks at me. Suddenly a pungent smoke swirl fills my senses and I am reminded that a chicken barbecue is being readied in a field behind the gas station. The tangy aroma of vinegar and sizzling chicken skin lures me in. The smoke becomes thicker. I turn to my right to ask Colleen if we have enough money to split a dinner. She is gone.* Fretfully, I awaken.

CHAPTER SEVEN

My next day of work was a nightmare. As soon as I got into the ward, Milkie appeared to have died. He was blue and lifeless. We were under strict orders to call Nurse Giles if he looked to be dead. Musty whisked Giles in so the baby could be taken back to Steiner in his dog-eared box. Polly arrived and was again agitated, looking for the baby. I put on some music to soothe her, but she stomped over to her chair and her rocking was fast and furious. She was inconsolable.

After lunch, Nurse Giles brought Milkie back to us.

"Baby X is in terminal prognosis now. Dr. Steiner is entertaining important physicians for a lunch engagement this afternoon and is unable to continue his research at this time. When the child expires, call agent Muskie and he will put him in a drawer down in the morgue. My shift is ending."

With that, she waddled away. Polly grabbed the box. She took Milkie for his last ride. About an hour later, I noticed Polly poking the baby. She sniffed the box.

I knew it was time. To make matters worse, Velmajean was working Birdie's shift. She abruptly snatched the box and paged Musty. Polly was beside herself. She stood up, looking as though she might charge at Velmajean. Musty appeared with a pistol drawn. The scene was absurd!

I stood in front of Polly so she couldn't see any more. She hopped up and down and then took to her rocker. Staff from her ward suddenly appeared with a nurse. She was restrained and given a shot. Staggering, with one staff member on each arm, she left in a drug-induced funk.

Milkie hadn't so much as cried or even opened his eyes. He had lain on his back in his boot box for his entire life, nearly motionless. He lived for fourteen days, a long life for someone born without a brain. He never once smiled. Yet in our recent game of musical chairs, he was included. We carried his box and danced around to the music. He wound up on the closest chair, and he won!

Milkie never responded to our reassuring words. But he looked content. Birdie had made him a small Christmas tree, which sat near his box during the holiday. A shimmering silver star dangled on the top of it.

Uncle Willie had once told me, "You do what you can for what you love. Don't matter if it is your Grandma or a three-legged cat. Don't matter if it is your neighbor down the road or a tree in your yard. Don't matter what it is. Could be a pumpkin growin' on the vine or your loyal dog. If there is love, you will do what you can. Ain't no mystery. Don't need no fancy words."

That night, I had a dream. *We are at the county fair on a sweltering summer day. Mom is chasing everyone around with suntan lotion. There is the usual familial indecisiveness about where to go next. Mom usually feigns sneezing when she is around pigs, goats, or chickens, so we are avoiding the barns. Each year, Dad announces that he is going to win super-sized stuffed animals for his best girls. The closest he has come is a half-dead goldfish, desperately trying to escape from a plastic bag. Colleen and I tell them that we are going to go to the midway for rides. We know full well that they won't want to go. We will meet them later, at the woodworking barn. We board the Electric Octopus. The thumping music blares away, astoundingly loud. The fair smells of sawdust and meat sitting on dirty grills. We are secured in our car by a smiling carnie worker flashing a gold tooth. The octopus shifts around slowly. As the arms go up and down, the cars at the ends of them begin to spin around. When Colleen and I are under stress, we laugh. We don't fidget or tap our feet; we giggle until we cry. We are laughing on the Electric Octopus. We get louder as the ride picks up speed. Our laughing mixes with the music. I close my eyes to feel the ride moving.* The dream ends.

An early January thaw had drained the earth of snow. The next day was colder, with a biting northerly wind. The Lake Erie snow machine had been turned on in narrow bands to the north of the mountains. Smokey Hollow was dry but cold. The wind stung and drew tears. The time had come to say goodbye to our Milkweed, Baby X. We were under strict orders to keep the burial brief. Special permission had been granted for Polly to be present. Dan had dug the baby a tiny rectangular grave in the cemetery. He brought the shoebox coffin out of the maintenance truck and placed it next to the grave. As he walked back to the truck, I quickly opened the box. The silver star from Birdie's Christmas tree was in my right pocket. I took it out and pushed it up under the baby's tube sock. I nervously closed the box because Milkie looked so cold. Just then, another pick-up pulled in and came up the lawn mowing path. Uncle Willie had agreed to play two songs to bid farewell.

Several crows, like pall-bearing sentries, fussed in a gray, skeletal tree. Restless and jittery, they argued and jockeyed for position. On cue, Willie distracted Dan with some weather talk. I quickly snuck over to Willie's truck and took out a small wooden box. I quietly dashed back to the grave and inserted it. This was Milkie's new coffin that Uncle Willie had made. I tucked the shoebox in it and closed the lid. My uncle had done some wood burning on the lid:

Baby Milkweed—Forever Loved
12/19/1976–1/2/1977

I helped Polly push in some dirt briskly so that no one would be the wiser. I felt a little bad about pulling this over on my friend

Dan. But I could not deprive the child of a proper casket. Willie sat on the back end of his messy pick-up and pulled out the fiddle. Polly and I stood at the grave. A sudden wind lifted old, loose leaves into the air, and they danced about while he played a mournful tune. We pushed the rest of the dirt into the grave. Willie played another sad song, which sounded Irish. I caught Dan crying to the melody while he pretended to get something from his truck. Frigid, stunned, and silent, I took Polly back to her ward.

In early February, Ward Four suffered a tragic fire. The siren sounded shortly after lunch and wailed all afternoon. Some of the residents were able to get out safely and were retrieved by staff from other wards. However, there were hideous screams from within, which I don't think I will ever forget. Windows were chopped out with axes, and the flames leaped into the air. Dan told me that one unfortunate soul jumped out a window with his clothes on fire. He landed in a snow bank. As the flames were extinguished, so was his life. In all, seven people died and nine were injured. Among the dead was Henry Joe Holloway, my smoking friend from the greenhouse. Word on the ward was that Musty had already pinned the fire on Henry. He said that the resident was a known arsonist who had killed his brother. Dan, on the other hand, told me that he saw Musty running frantically from the building like a scared child. This happened just before the alarm was pulled. The thought that the Chief of Security saved himself before others made me cringe. The cause of the fire, according to my friend Donnie Wayne Briggs, was "careless smoking."

Dan, who rarely became angry, let loose.

"The f-f-fire started in the d-d-downstairs office. Henry wouldn't h-h-have been in the office, ever! They weren't even allowed on that f-f-floor."

"You need to tell the police, Dan."

"And l-l-lose my j-j-job? Steiner has already ordered that the b-b-building be d-d-demolished. All the evidence will be g-g-gone."

"People died, Dan! The least you can do is tell the police. This will tear you up for the rest of your life if you don't do something."

I offered to go to the police with him. He told me he would think about it one more night.

After work the next day, I walked part way down the hill, and Dan picked me up there. We didn't want to be seen riding together, so I crouched down in the front of his pick-up. We pulled up behind the State Police barracks and went in the back. We went in separately with winter hats pulled down tightly. In a small town, someone is always watching. I told the officer at the desk that we needed to talk to someone about a possible crime. I went in first, but as I had no real firsthand knowledge other than the grass fire, I was sent back to the waiting room. Dan was gone at least a half hour or so. He came out sweaty and flushed because he had left his wool hat on the whole time. As silence is sometimes the best ointment, we didn't speak. Dan left me off behind the school bus garage and I walked home in the dark.

I dreamed that we were back at the county fair. *Colleen and I break away from the family. We are on the midway again. A young girl is running in loose flip flops. She trips over a cable and drops her candied apple. Screaming and red faced, she is mourning her shattered sugary treat, which is quickly attracting ants. My sister and I try the fun house, where, according to the sign, "all hell breaks loose." There are those hokey distortion mirrors and some other lame surprises. We move on to Madame Aurora's tent. According to the recorded message, she will, "stare at your soul and reveal it to you, all for 50 cents."*

"Well, that seems worth the money!"

Colleen winks at me.

I sit with Madame Aurora, who is wearing a black eye patch and smells of cigars. She has a gold turban sitting atop her head and is wearing many bracelets and rings. While she is "staring at my soul," she turns suddenly to Colleen.

"Young lady, you must be very careful. The black cat has crossed your path." The dream ends.

I had a vague remembrance of playing with someone named

Holloway when we would sneak up to Uncle Willie's, so I called him.

"Yes, there was a Duane Holloway who would come by when you was a youngin'. They was hill folk who had an outhouse."

"Do you know anything about a fire up there?"

"There was a fire in the barn and one of their boys died out there. I think he went out to feed the animals. There was a bad storm, so talk was that there was a lightnin' strike. He's buried up at Heavenly Gate Graveyard, where I tend the mowing."

"Do you know anything about them now? Are any of them still around? Henry just died in the Smokey Hollow fire."

"Ain't that odd! Duane still lives out near Crabapple Run. He ain't the friendliest thing, and I hear it told that he has taken a few shots at strangers. Tammy Jo is somewhere in town. She married someone named Bingham or Bigham. He runs the feed store and she works there, too."

I went in and bought some bird seed from Tammy Jo Bigham. But I couldn't bring myself to say anything else. I wasn't sure what to say anyway. I remembered Juanita Lyons and my pledge that I wasn't to say anything about the people who lived at Smokey Hollow. It wouldn't have been a very good introduction to tell her that her brother was probably sent away for no good reason and that people still thought he killed little Homer. Added to that story, Henry was being blamed for the deaths of his fellow residents, too. I guess sometimes it's best not to know what other people think, especially when all the news is bad. I went up to Heavenly Gate Graveyard and found the Holloway boy's grave. He was memorialized by a little lamb. Once white, it was grey and worn, and the carved little face had more or less been eradicated by time. Homer had died on June 6, 1964.

From there, I rode my bike to the town library. Behind the desk was Verna Lou Vaughn from our church. She was notoriously nosey and bossy, so it was going to be difficult to get what I needed without her nipping at my heels. I requested the town newspapers for 1964. Verna Lou reminded me that there was only 45 minutes left before closure. She then started what seemed to be a 45-minute lecture on rules for "special collections," which included, "absolutely no chewing gum, no leaning on the books, no colored ink, fingernails must be clean and trimmed, pages must be turned slowly and completely, and blah, blah, blah…." At last, I was allowed to cross into the special collection area, which was really just a table in front of some old books. Verna Lou dramatically presented me with the large volume while she wore white gloves. Luckily, another patron started ringing Verna Lou's little bell impatiently. As soon as she left, I quickly got to work. I found Homer's obituary.

LITTLE HOMER HOLLOWAY PERISHES IN FIRE

"Residents of the Blackberry Run area were shocked Saturday evening by the loss of little Homer Holloway, aged eight. The young lad was discovered in the charred remains of a barn on the Holloway farm. A pony and some chickens also died. The cause of the fire is under investigation. He is survived by his parents, Mr. and Mrs. Perry Holloway; sisters Grace Marie, Tammy Jo, and Darlene; brothers Henry, Perry Jr., Ricky, and Duane. Graveside services will be held at Heavenly Gate on Tuesday morning at 9:00 a.m. Rev. Harley Jones will officiate."

I paged through the papers, turning slowly and completely. I saw grocery store ads for, Big Al's Market in town. Amazingly, in the "Send a Bouquet" column, I found this little tidbit:

"Miss Lorna Tillman is recovering at home after suffering a heat spell at the church picnic. During the chicken barbecue, she took on a feverish pallor. Despite all efforts to fan and cool her, she was rushed to the hospital where she is recovering from dehydration. Visitors and cards are welcome."

I laughed to myself! I pictured my aunt, being fanned like Cleopatra with leftover paper plates. I saw those who knew her continuing on with their meal, eating their blackened chicken and coleslaw. Just another day in the life of Lorna! I turned another page and on the back page of an issue from late July was this article:

FREAK LIGHTNING STRIKE CAUSED HOLLOWAY FIRE
"Previously suspected to have been deliberately set, the fire that killed little Homer Holloway was caused by an unusual lightning strike on the property on the night of June 6. Several neighbors have confirmed this, and investigators discovered evidence on the scene."

I tried writing it all down but heard Verna Lou fast approaching. I had found all that I needed. Musty was a liar. I wondered about Henry. Was he sent to the hollow before this article came out? Were his "deficiencies" noticed before or after the inferno?

That night, I drifted off into a dream. *We are back at the county fair. Joey DiStefano has come with us. My mother is bothered by the humidity and sore feet. Dad sits forlorn, eyeing the beer tent. Joey and Colleen look at each other, non-verbally communicating their desire to ditch the family. They leave me to tend to the parents. Dad complains about prices. "The fair? Well, it sure isn't fair! Nothing but a rip-off!" I gave them an hour of alone time and walk the midway. There are loud, rhythmic songs competing with the huge, grinding rides. People go up and down, here and there. Grown men scream like babies and pee their pants slightly. Teenage girls, strutting in cowgirl boots, dig their nails into each other as the rides rise and fall, back and forth. And, everyone yells in fear and anticipation. I stop to see the "Zombie Girl from the Jungle of Haiti." The barker calls from in front of her tent.*

> *"She rose from her dirt-filled grave*
> *She rose from the land of the dead*
> *She'll scream and rant and rave*
> *She'll fill your dreams with dread."*

Her eyes widened, the "zombie" begins to murmur in what sounds like French. Suddenly, she screams. Her blood-curdling voice is piercing the thick summer air. As she shakes her head, dirt falls around her. As I exit the tent, I see Polly walking ahead. Her hair is pulled back into some kind of ponytail. I am running up to catch up to her. I get snagged in a gathering of slow-moving parents, burdened with baby buggies and wandering toddlers. I look ahead and Polly is gone. I can't see where she went. Sweating and panting, I look everywhere. I am awake again.

CHAPTER EIGHT

In early April, I noticed a sign in our shabby ward office that promoted the annual Easter parade. A mimeographed paper contained a childish drawing of a rabbit carrying a basket of eggs. I was unclear as to how Easter took precedence over the rotten institutional Christmas. The December holiday season had been punctuated with additional gravy on the mashed potatoes. Santa had arrived after dinner to pass out socks and underwear. Reeking of vodka, he fell asleep mid-way through the festivities. When awoken and asked to leave, he became belligerent, swearing loudly as the record player played "Oh Holy Night."

I was encouraged that this parade would allow us to get out into the fresh air and sunshine. The dreary wards were confining and miserable. The furniture was mismatched. Polly's new rocker was a pukey pink color. Her old maple rocker had collapsed one day. The spindles separated from the seat one by one and then *wham*! There she was, laughing on the floor surrounded by her old chair. In further decorative irony, she usually rocked under a huge rainbow, spray painted on the wall. Even that source of "eternal inspiration" was tinged with rust stains and peeling.

Parade day arrived. Each person was given a plastic headband with two, egg carton ears attached. Some of the residents of another ward had cut egg cartons lengthwise and tied them to the bands. Vina immediately tossed hers to the floor. It wasn't worth the struggle. Vina was good at expressing her likes and dislikes, and there was no point in revisiting things when she had already made her statement. If we had handed it to her a second time, she likely would have given the whole works a good stomping. We went up to the circular driveway to await the festivities. Those who managed to keep on their rabbit ears looked shockingly ridiculous, more like insects with antennae sprouting out of their heads.

Little huddles of people waited and there were more were lined up to march. I was never really clear how many people lived at the Holler because we were so isolated from the rest of the residents. Birdie thought that there were at least a few hundred who lived on the grounds. One ward had a group of bunny hoppers. Some sang the song, and a staff person blew a whistle when it was time to hop. While it certainly wasn't performed in unison, they seemed to be enjoying the attention and applause. The bunny ears took more tragic tumbles as several were jarred loose during all the jumping.

There was a troop of clowns, carrying Easter colored balloons. Two of them rode on unicycles. One was unable to keep the cycle balanced, and she tipped over. Her blue wig fell off and breezily rolled along the parade route like a tumble weed until someone stepped on it and returned it to her. Some of the residents carried a large American flag. They were followed by a large calliope, which sounded like it was playing "Easter Parade" under water.

In one of my most bizarre moments in my Smokey Hollow career, Officer Musty slowly followed the circus organ in his gumball wagon. And he was dressed up! He seemed to be a cross between a hobo and a clown. He bore a strong resemblance to "Freddie the Freeloader." His permanent frown was accentuated by his clown make-up. Musty was a bum who was finally dressed for the part. I had begun to look him directly in the eye after the fire. I mouthed words like "arsonist" and "murderer." Dan had warned me to stop, but I didn't.

The Easter lunch was another globby mound that best resembled scalloped potatoes. The food there was so bland and easy to swallow. Choking was always a concern, so the food was frequently scooped into lifeless lumps. Ground ham and mushy carrots were stuck within the potato mixture, giving it a color similar to cat food. Meat was never served in its true form or texture. It was ground, chopped, or otherwise pulverized. Even dessert—banana pudding for Easter—came in a gelatinous ball.

At home, springtime brought some improvements with Mom. She got outside occasionally to her gardens. Despite all that had happened in the family, her bulbs had poked their heads up, with the crocuses emerging first through the dirty leftover snow. They were followed in the traditional sequence by daffodils, tulips, and irises.

"I had almost forgotten how beautiful my gardens were. Colleen, as a girl, would pick a flower a day for me for most of the spring and summer. She always called it my 'One a day Vitamin.' Each one went into a vase next to the kitchen window."

"Well, let's do it, Mom." I cut a couple of flowers, which she carefully put on display in exactly the same spot. I noticed that she added some from time to time. When I remembered, I would do the same.

Dad still talked to the television on a frequent basis, but he seemed to be taking a little better care of himself. He had resumed his "B and B Thursdays," bowling and beer at Gutterball Sally's. I considered it a victory whenever they left the house. With so many reminders of Colleen in the house, it was almost as if they were paralyzed whenever they stayed within it for too long. Mom had moved Colleen's boots into the basement. Beyond that, they hadn't touched any of her things for close to six months.

Mom said, "When Colleen comes back, everything will be just as she had left it".

I hoped that she was right.

That night, vivid images filled my dreaming mind. *Our Uncle has taken all of us kids to Thistle Creek. We are in the creek looking for Allegheny alligators or, as Uncle Willie calls them, hellbenders. They are huge, pre-historic–looking salamanders that hide under rocks. Rita and I have discovered that they like to eat small crayfish, so we are catching them in a little net and setting them loose under a large rock. The crayfish are disappearing in the murky abyss. I am getting ready to give it my best shot and grab for one of the slippery critters. I plunge my hand in, but we are all suddenly distracted by Kevy's return from downstream. He looks like he is on the verge of crying and his cheek seems swollen. Willie asks him what happened.*

Blinking back tears, he says, "I was chased by a swarm of bees and one stung me under my eye. I tripped and cut me knee."

"Jesus, boy, you are a mess. Come here."

Willie pulls out the stinger and tells Kevy that he should sit still for a minute. Our Uncle dabs some mud paste on Kevy's reddened cheek.

"Boy, did you step on a dead animal or something?"

"I fell after I got stung. There are some weird plants in there."

"You must have kicked over some skunk cabbage. You'll have to ride in the back on the way home."

Realizing his insult, Willie quickly rubbed Kevy's hair to keep the tears from erupting again. Suddenly, the dream had ended.

I called Donnie Wayne Briggs and asked him if he wanted to have lunch with me. My meeting with Curran had yielded nothing but hard feelings and more frustration. I turned to Donnie Wayne to see if he knew anything else about Colleen's sudden departure. He swung by in his gumball-topped pick-up. We had decided to head up the Raccoon River to the Peregrine Roost, a new restaurant about twenty miles away.

Donnie Wayne started, "I have to tell you that Colleen's disappearance is a mystery, and my Dad looks and listens for clues wherever he goes. We are really sorry for you and your family. What is it like?"

"It is hell, DW. It is absolute hell. It's like we did something wrong but we don't even know what we did. I just want to rewind and go back in time. We think of new ways to try to find her, but it just never happens. I wake up from dreams, write them down, and re-read them over and over to see if there is a clue somewhere within. Life is nothing but questions without answers. We relive moments over and over, trying to remember anything that we may have missed. People have long left us to wallow in our own misery. They look away uncomfortably or stare when we aren't looking. With the day to day stress of the unknown, I haven't even had time to realize how much I miss her. I know it sounds strange, but if Colleen were helping me, I have often thought that we would have already found her."

And just like that, one of my most poignant moments was gone as the waitress fretfully delivered our meatloaf sandwiches.

CHAPTER NINE

Rita and I went to see Detective Wally Banks. The portly officer came out to find us a good fifteen minutes after we had arrived. He attempted to tidy up his messy little hovel as we followed him in. After some dramatic sighing and shuffling of papers and portfolios, he cleared two seats for us. A Donut Delight box was flipped open, the top stained with oily spots. There were old Styrofoam coffee cups and newer ones strewn about. He picked up a folder and started describing all he had done to find our sister, Sherilyn. Rita and I exchanged a glance and I interrupted him.

"Who is Sherilyn? She isn't our sister!"

With that, he started fumbling around on his disorderly desk. As his face became flushed, he nervously told us extensive details about Sherilyn's disappearance. He referenced her abusive husband who also had gone missing, leaving behind a six-year-old boy.

"You have to feel bad about the kid. Damn shame."

Buried under some notebooks was Colleen's folder, adorned with coffee-stained rings.

"Ah, yes, here it is. I was just looking this over today. We have interviewed everyone who was mentioned as possibly having more information. We have no new leads. We don't know if your sister came into harm's way. While we found her purse, there was nothing else to indicate that she had been harmed. We conducted a thorough search of Sandstone Creek. Is it possible that she just left town for a while?"

"No, we would have heard from her by now. She would have called or written. Why would her purse have been at the river if she left town?"

"Well, you never know with these kids nowadays. She could have met up with some hippies. A lot of them are on drugs."

With that, I exploded. As I rose, my army coat cuff got snagged on the donut box, and it fell to the floor. Like a madman, I stomped on the box. I jumped on it several times, smashing donuts and shooting rivulets of berry jelly and custard cream all over his stained little desk.

"You don't know anything! You never did!"

Rita seemed to recognize that I was going a tad berserk in a police station. She rose, apologized, and prodded me toward the door. Once we were a safe distance away, we doubled up on cigarettes. I swore profusely, and Rita referred to the detective as a "soiled incompetent." If we were to find Colleen, it was obvious that we were on our own.

Up at Smokey Hollow, I had been teaching Gary how to feed himself. Uncle Willie had fashioned him a little leather strap that would around his hand once he had the spoon in place. The first few times he lost quite a bit of food but he was got better at it with time. He learned how to balance the spoon and aim for his mouth. Birdie and I often wondered how much more the kids could have done for themselves had they been taught at an early age. I guess Velmajean got wind of my work with Gary. One day, she told me that it was urgent that I see her before I left. She presented me with a written warning. It read something like this: "Employee is providing patient with unauthorized instruction, void of clinical advice. Employee is creating false hope for patient. Conduct of this nature must cease immediately or employee may be transferred or terminated."

"You got any questions? If not, you need to sign there, 'neath where Dr. Steiner signed."

"I just have one question."

Looking impatient and annoyed, she hissed and crossed her arms. "Well, what is it then?"

"Velmajean, can you please provide me with a definition of false hope?" As I frequently did when stressed, I began laughing. I signed her little form and wrote on the bottom, "Gary was so proud of himself." I asked her for a photocopy, which she later angrily slammed onto the table.

False hope was the definition of Smokey Hollow. It was the land of betrayal and intrusion. Birdie and I had begun asking about education and therapies. We begged for supplies and activities. We brought in flea market books and read to the children. One of the few times that Vina would sit and join the group was when I read during story hour. Birdie said that it probably reminded her of a happier time. Perhaps someone in her family had read to her. Birdie often made afghans and blankets for the kids. Soon, they would be sent off to the laundry and then we never saw them again. Birdie once ran into Velmajean's daughter at the grocery store. There, in her baby's stroller, was one of Birdie's handmade creations. Birdie told me that the daughter exhaled after a drag on her cigarette and said, "Is there somethin' wrong with you, lady? Mind your business and quit staring at my kid."

Back at Smokey Hollow, things were deteriorating. Nurse Giles marched in one morning and announced that she was conducting "routine physicals." I asked that we use a privacy screen so the kids had some dignity. Obviously unhappy to have an attendant suggesting such an accommodation, she insisted that nearly everyone be restrained or sedated. I told her that most of the kids would comply if we just gave them some time. Seemingly even angrier, her busy little syringe of Thorazine went to work. The kids were poked and prodded by this little tree trunk of a nurse. After numerous fits of screaming, painful sedation, and unnecessarily rough treatment, she took her little black bag of goodies and left. Vina attempted to bite the nurse in the ear, but I was able to calm her down. I wrote a letter to Dr. Steiner, complaining specifically about Nurse Giles. In response, I received another written warning for "interfering with required medical procedures." I added it to my growing dossier of trouble. Polly's ward staff called and announced that she would be gone for the summer. They said that her family was moving from Puerto Rico to Florida, and they wanted to spend some time with her. This made little sense to me, as Birdie had told me that Polly had been abandoned as a newborn and left on a step of a convent. I called her ward to get her "summer address" so we could send her a birthday card in July. That staff member referred me to the administrative building and Dr. Steiner. I ran into my friend Dan as I was leaving and told him that I needed some important information. I mentioned that I had been written up and that I needed his help.

"I just need to know Steiner's schedule. Can you find out when he will be going away?"

"I t-t-told you to be c-c-careful.

"OK, Dan, just do a little snooping around for me, will you? I just need to know when he will be out of town."

Dan shifted from side to side uneasily.

"J-j-j-just k-k-k-keep it all quiet."

"Dan, would you want your mother to live here? Or your niece?

"N-n-no."

"There is your answer, then."

I had another dream. *We are in the church hall. We are eating corned beef and leeks. We are a captive audience as Reverend Hinckley carries on about Satanic messages sent through guitars. He specifically references Alice Cooper and Led Zeppelin. Colleen and I are laughing. We have learned from experience that our laughter will only get louder, so we have to split up. She dashes away for the ladies room. Suddenly, the overhead lights go down. A curtain and center stage is filled with a huge wooden cross. It is festooned with large yellow Christmas lights. A spotlight cranks overhead as a line of young women emerge from behind the cross. There is a catwalk of sorts, and it looks like either a fashion show or a beauty pageant. One woman resembles Colleen, but when she gets closer, I see that it is not her. And then, out comes Polly, smiling broadly. She is suffering from a heavy dose of five o'clock shadow. She waves to me and flashes her unmistakable mismatched peg teeth. She wanders about the stage, rocking forward and back. The yellow cross begins blinking on and off.*

Somewhere in the unknown space between dreams and reality, I became aware of the jingling telephone. No one in the house was awake, so I ran to the kitchen and picked it up. I noticed that the clock said 4:00 a.m. Only half awake, I heard something about the State Police so quickly rousted Mom and Dad. Rita must not have heard the commotion. My heart raced. I knew that this was finally the call we had been waiting for. At last, we would know more about my sister. It was hard to wait! Dad took the phone. I guess it was presumed then that Dads know how to take bad news better. He mumbled little phrases such as "uh-hum" and "Yes. I see." He hung up.

"Sorry to have to tell you that Lorna was found dead in the bathtub. A neighbor heard her dog howling. The police suspect that she was changing a cassette and the whole player fell into the tub."

My anger, quicker to flare up than usual, was unbridled. I slammed the door to my room. Briefly, like a summer thunderstorm, I wept. I couldn't believe this was happening now. I thought for sure the call would have been about Colleen. Now the family focus would shift again. Lorna's life of sickness and misery would take center stage. Even from a cold drawer in the morgue, she would dominate the family headlines again. And Colleen's sad, unknown fate would fade further into obscurity. I wrote Rita a brief note and slid it under her door before I left for work. Mom had left me a message on the fridge. "Please stop at your aunt's house on the way home. Something will need to be done with her dog. Thanks." I called Uncle Willie when I got to work, but even he declined the dog.

"Little dogs take on more of their owner's habits, and believe me, I ain't got room for all that over here."

I pulled up to Lorna's house and immediately heard little Elvis the King barking. When the real Elvis had died on the toilet the previous summer, poor Lorna had gone into mourning. Her grieving included excessive consumption of chips and dip. She ordered large tins of Crunch Master Crinkles from Big Al's grocery store. She complemented the chips with tubs of sour cream. Dipping and crunching, she played Elvis music into the dark. Once her exploitation of his death had worn off, she had a short-lived nervous breakdown. Then, she went out and got her dog, the King. Always antsy and jumpy, little Elvis spun in circles like a whirling dervish. He was well known for his accidents, peeing and pooping whenever the mood struck him. I let myself into the house, and the King started yipping and dancing. Lorna's house had belonged to my grandparents. They had left it to her in their will. Mom often said that this was because "she hadn't found the right man yet." Colleen and I had naughtily developed a list of qualities that "the right man" would have required. It was a long list! We had laughed so hard, we started to cry. Lorna's house smelled of King and his little "mistakes." I hadn't been inside the house in years. To console herself during her numerous bouts of disease and dysfunction, she collected porcelain figurines. Ironically, the little dolls were usually little children, carefree with whimsical little smiles. When Lorna went "lipstick manic" as my mother said, she told Colleen that "makeup is the only way to paint a smile over my sadness." Dad, on the other hand, referred to these periods as "going lipstick dipstick."

Elvis followed me as I took one pass through the house. I stopped at the bathroom. On the sink was a small plastic box full of cassette tapes by the Carpenters and the Captain and Tennille. Her undies were still on the hamper, so I added all of that to the kitchen garbage and took it to the outside can. I suddenly felt a wave of sadness for Lorna. I don't know why. I just couldn't imagine dying as you were reaching to hear "We've Only Just Begun" or "Love Will Keep Us Together." What tragic irony. I found the King's food and put him in a picnic basket I found in the garage. He came home with me, his basket wired up to my bicycle Toto style. When I got home, I put him in the basement laundry room until we could find a permanent owner.

The next evening, I took Mom to the Perry and Logan Funeral

Home. The undertaker, old Harold Perry, limped out to greet us with his sales pitch of death.

"You will want a nice spray of roses for the coffin. I assume. Some families spend more on 'top of the line' coffins if the deceased had not made their plans ahead of time."

Mr. Perry took out a pipe, filled it with tobacco, and fired up. As the nicotine began to nibble at his brain, his ideas expanded.

"From my records here, I see that the Tillman plot is still unmarked. This is a good time to start considering a respectable memorial for your loved ones. Here is a card for Ralph Dundee at Dundee Monuments. You will want to give him a call soon because I think he is still running his summer special."

I interrupted. "What is a summer special? Is that like two for one? Or buy one get one free?"

With noticeable indifference, Perry took another deep drag and released black cherry smoke, bluish in tinge.

"Young man, day in and day out, we comfort the bereaved here. And this is a one horse town. I am here to help you with your choices."

Mom, dejected and fidgeting with her purse, said that she needed some air. She promised to call the parlor in the morning with her decisions. We left. After a prolonged silence backed up by the rhythm of the windshield wipers, she said, "Services will be private. My baby girl Colleen is God knows where. Lorna was a grifter who stole my parents blind and left their beautiful home smelling of dogs. I can't deal with this. There will be no spray of roses. She had hundreds of bouquets throughout her life, and none of them did a damn thing to improve her mood. God help me for what I have said, but I will never be taken for a fool again as long as I live."

Lorna's service was held briefly at the graveside. She joined her parents in the yet-unmarked Tillman family plot. Mom's Aunt Ruth and cousin Lucille rolled their eyes frequently. After the service, Lucille approached my father.

"My elderly mother and I drove a half hour to listen to a snake-handling preacher mumble a few prayers? To top it off, we aren't even offered a sandwich or proper tureen? I don't even know why we came."

Dad, not often known for witty comebacks, said, "I don't know either."

When we got home, I found a foil-covered dish full of Uncle Willie's signature macaroni and cheese. There was a bouquet of wildflowers in a an empty whiskey bottle, and he had written "sorry for y'all" on the label.

My mother said, "Good Lord, couldn't he have found a vase? I hope the neighbors didn't see this!"

Birdie was kind enough to find a neighbor to adopt little Elvis. Her sister had been ill a lot, requiring her to take time off from work. Velmajean took offense at that and wrote her up as well. I honestly thought that Velmajean hated the fact that Birdie and I got along well. I guess miserable people are like rabid dogs, as Dan had once told me. Their only goal is to infect others with their unhappiness.

I ran into Dan that week and reminded him that I wanted to know Dr. Steiner's schedule. I told him that I needed important information from the administration building.

"I'll f-f-find out what I c-c-can. Be c-c-careful. Your job will be on the l-l-line."

"It already is, Danno." In honor of Hawaii Five-O, Dan's favorite T.V. show, I had bestowed him with that nickname.

That night, I had another dream. *Uncle Willie has taken Colleen and I camping. Our tents are set up on the outskirts of his property. He has created a huge bonfire in the fire pit. Twigs snap and pop as the inferno starts. The sweet smell of smoking pine fills the air. We are sitting on uneven tree stumps. Willie has prepared a meal especially for us. He cut up hot dogs and threw them into canned baked beans. We pass around a bag of potato chips, a forbidden food at our family dinner table. The flames dance as Uncle Willie plays his fiddle. Later, in the tent, I hear the calls of the pond frogs. Their loud, bellowing communication is rhythmic and reassuring. They sound like giant rubber bands. Crickets create the contra-rhythm.*

Suddenly, I am back outside, sliding into dew-tinged sneakers. Colleen hears me and comes out as well. Hootie, Willie's owl, flies in carrying some strange mythological prey. Poe flies in for a stand-off. There is a grotesque fight, and Poe goes for Hootie's eye. While Hootie has far greater range of motion in his neck, Poe is the smaller bird. It is the smaller bird that can chase the larger one, knowing that it can't quickly turn around. Suddenly, the tents catch fire, and we are on the run. Uncle Willie leads us with a flashlight. Poe sits on his shoulder with a crimson beak. Colleen is behind me. And, then, I no longer hear her running behind me. I turn around and she is gone. I sit down on a grassy mound, waiting. I run back toward the fire. I turn right and left. I can't find her.

Then, I am in a barn. There is a pony with a matted mane and hens wandering around aimlessly. There is a boy in ripped blue jeans scattering cracked corn for the chickens. Suddenly, there is an earth-shattering thud and a crackling overhead. The boy, drained of color, lies in the hay and wriggles and writhes about like a caterpillar flipped on its back. Fire licks at the roof first. Once it has gobbled up the top of the barn, it rapidly descends, destroying everything. Brilliant purple embers fall downward and the hay is lit. The chickens squawk and fly onto each other as their space shrinks. The pony bucks and cries until it is overcome by smoke. I run away, not remembering who I was looking for in the first place. I run and run, but I am not sure where I am going. Then, I am on the grounds of Smokey Hollow. I am looking frantically for Dan. He is not in his usual places, so I keep running. While I am still outside, it seems to be getting warmer somehow. All of the sudden it is hot. I am outside Ward Four, and it is engulfed in flames. Distant sirens wail as fire trucks slowly wind up Asylum Road. The smoke is thick and suffocating. The brilliant flames are mesmerizing as they leap before me. I am paralyzed and unable to move. And then, I am awake, heart racing, destination unknown.

CHAPTER TEN

In May, Birdie called me early one morning. She spoke anxiously. She told me that she had heard that a fourteen-year-old girl was missing from the Sunflower Hill Mobile Home Park. According to Birdie's neighbor, the girl's mother became concerned when her daughter didn't get up for school. The bedroom revealed an empty bed and an open window. Birdie didn't have any other details but promised to keep us informed as she got more news.

Immediately intrigued, I turned on the radio to wait for some local news reports. Station WXYZ played country and western music by day and hard rock at night. I listened to a few twangy songs and an ad for a Memorial Day tractor pull. At last, the news crackled through.

"Local police are asking the public to be on the alert for a missing teenager from the Sunflower Hill area. Fourteen-year-old Dorena Ann Devoe is five feet, two inches tall and has long black hair. Anyone who has information about her should call Detective Wallace Banks."

I had gone to elementary school with a Dale Devoe and thought this could be his sister. I couldn't recall him from high school so assumed that the family had moved away. Dale had been a quiet kid whose eyes seemed permanently downcast. I knew little of his family but had assumed that is was a hardscrabble lot. He brought little for lunch, so I had often let him mooch from me. We had an unspoken agreement that I would pass him food under the table so no one else would know.

I couldn't help but wonder if Dorena's disappearance was related in some way to my missing sister. I began to obsess over it. I called Birdie several times. I kept the radio on and turned the volume up whenever the news came on. The report went unchanged. Rita had joined me in my radio vigil after I told her what had happened. In an effort to pass the time, her "poet self" became quite critical of the country lyrics.

"Listen to these things! These men mourn their mommas, dogs, and pick-up trucks. They rarely mention the women who clean their toilets or carry their twelve-packs in from the store."

"I know, Rita. They've been wronged a thousand times over! They whine away about rough weeks at work, hangovers, and lost poker games. I can't wait for the switchover to hard rock!"

Rita suggested that we go to the Devoe house the following day. While I thought it was a good idea, it provoked anxiety. As welcoming as some homes seem in a small town, there are just as many with "BEWARE OF THE DOG!" or "NO TRESPASSING!" signs. Sunflower Hill was a wagon wheel of mobile homes. Visiting a family in crisis brought many risks. But my overwhelming desire to see if there was any connection to Colleen overruled my nagging doubts.

Rita and I stopped at Big Al's grocery to get some food for the Devoe family. We loitered at the bakery and debated about what to get. We finally decided on a blueberry pie and an almond ring. We put the white boxes on the back seat and began our drive up Sunflower Hill. We passed some working farms and a couple that looked long abandoned. Sunflower Hill Road was steep and rutted. I had to swerve around the carcass of an unidentifiable animal. Swarming with flies and maggots, the bloody mess was strewn all over the road. Two guilty looking crows sat nearby, waiting to hop and nibble when the car passed. Rita and I rolled up the windows as the gaseous odors of death had suddenly filled the car. A couple of miles later, the almond ring had warmed up in the sun and brought us sweet relief.

I turned into the mobile home park. A long-neglected garden was at the center of the circular arrangement of trailers. There were a few droopy sunflowers, weeds, and a rogue sumac tree. A bearded man in a sleeveless tee shirt sat in a lawn chair. Loud music poured out of his trailer while he feigned air guitar. I slowed down and asked if he knew the Devoes.

"Three up on the left. The girl turned up missin' so they is pretty shook up!"

We passed a mobile home in which a Confederate flag served as a window treatment. The Devoe mobile home was just past it. Rita carried the baked goods while I knocked on the screen door. A dog barked, and a female voice could be heard shrieking.

"Dale, lock the damn dog up. There is someone at the door! Corky, shut yer fat mouth!"

After some door slamming and dog whining, Dale Devoe came to the door. He was the same person I remembered from school, but I didn't mention it. I explained who we were and that we brought some food out of concern. He looked down frequently and didn't seem to know what to say.

"Now we is all upset here. I just don't know what y'all want."

Rita said, "We just want you to know that we care. And with our sister being missing for months, we hope to bring them both home."

With that, he brushed back a quick tear and went inside. He had a muffled conversation with a person with a motherly tone.

"We don't know these people. Tell them they can come in for a couple minutes, but that's it."

Dale sheepishly let us in and we walked into a paneled living area. His mother sat in a well-worn recliner. It was obvious that the television console was her nerve center. A box of Kleenex sat next to an open bag of potato chips. There were empty soda bottles perched precariously next to a large ashtray. The room was stale, like the inside of an old suitcase. Mrs. Devoe wore a housecoat and slippers. Her hair was tightly wound around pink plastic rollers, giving her face a pinched appearance. Rita nervously presented the food boxes to her. She seemed to soften a bit.

"Dale, where is your manners? This girl has a fresh berry pie here. Put it in the kitchen by the bread box."

She asked us to sit on a long-suffering sofa. It was matted with animal hair and reeked of a wet dog. I told her briefly about Colleen.

"I think I seen heard about her. Dale, didn't you say that you knew her family?"

"Yes, ma'am."

"Well, Jesus, where is your manners? You know these here folks?"

"Yes, ma'am. I know him from grade school."

"Well, put some of those chips in a bowl for them then. My son has cracked his head a few times so you will have to excuse him. He never did finish school hisself."

Mrs. Devoe quickly explained that Dorena took the bus back and forth to school. She said that Dorena's only close friend was Lena Lumpkin, and, that she sometimes spent the night at the Lumpkin home.

"We ain't exactly the Rockefellers, so I don't know why those Lumpkins took to Dorena. Probably just felt sorry for her, I guess. Ain't no other reason they'd be with our kind."

Our visit ended abruptly when the phone rang. Dale tried his best to deal with the call, but his mother interrupted. She promised she would call us if she thought of anything else.

Dale took us to the door. As we slid into the car, Mrs. Devoe could be heard from within the trailer.

"Dale, I am talkin' here with your Aunt Lynette. Mind your

manners and cut me a big slice of that berry pie. I hope there is still a can of whipped cream in there, too."

Three days later, the battered and bruised body of little Dorena Ann Devoe was found in the Raccoon River woods. Donnie Wayne Briggs called me and said that she was discovered by a woman walking her dog. Reportedly, her eyes were swollen purple and there was evidence that she had been strangled. Her murder sent shock waves through the town. I was suddenly filled with incredible anger. Had this been the fate of my beautiful sister? What kind of monster would kill a young girl? Who was the beast who could punch a helpless teen in the eyes?

The day after Dorena's remains were found, the town was on fire with rumors. There was midday talk that Larry Lumpkin had gone missing. Someone in Aunt Jennie's Diner said that they saw him jump off the river bridge. Donnie Wayne called me and said that Larry had been questioned at length about Dorena Devoe. His father had updated us on the situation and said that Faith Lumpkin had reported her husband as missing.

A search ensued for Larry Lumpkin, hard-working head of the church choir and possible murder suspect. Plagued by mosquitoes and poison ivy, those looking for him soon dwindled in numbers. Most in town had already heard about the police interview. A sudden burst of summer heat led even more to abandon the search.

Bloated and pasty, Larry Lumpkin's corpse shook free of the river bed and rose to the surface like a human balloon. Donnie Wayne told me that the crick critters had made off with his eyes. A fisherman found the body.

It was indeed a busy month at the Perry and Logan Funeral Parlor. Dorena had an hour-long wake and service immediately thereafter. Rita and I went. Mrs. Devoe had taken to a wheelchair. She was visibly distraught.

"For days, the church ladies have been in and out of that Lumpkin house, takin' in their covered dishes. Dale seen them. Just like ants on a birthday cake. This is what Christians do? My baby was murdered and thrown into the weeds like a sack of trash. And these Christians with their noses in the air go into the house of a murderer? They have some misplaced notions!"

Rita was a voice of reason.

"Ma'am, we are so sorry for your suffering. We can only imagine how upset you must be. Dorena was a beautiful girl, and we hope that you will always see her that way. We have some food for you and your family in the car."

"Thank you, young lady. I'm glad someone in this town cares. Dale, mind your manners! These nice folks brought some food. Now, see that it gets into the truck."

I went out of the funeral home with Dale. There was Harold Perry, stuck in a chair, oblivious to everything except his tobacco. Smoke swirled above him.

Dale looked down and said, "I never did thank you for givin' me food when we was in grade school. We had no money after my Dad ran off. Somedays, I was near starvin.'"

"You don't have to thank me."

"Well, I am, damnit! I have been hushed and shushed my whole life. So why don't you stop treating me like I am less in your eyes and let me say thank you."

"I am sorry. You're welcome."

Dale transferred the food to his truck, and Rita and I bid him goodbye.

The very next day, Larry Lumpkin's coffin was placed on the same spot in which Dorena had rested the night before. Donnie Wayne Briggs sat in his truck across the street to take note of the comings and goings. While there were callers from the church choir and scouts, he told me that the wake was poorly attended. I asked Donnie why he would sit there, and he said he had been looking for clues to try and figure out if Larry was connected to the murder. I guess Donnie didn't want to admit that he was perpetually on the lookout for scandalous scuttlebutt.

My mother, a semi-professional mourner, had begun fretting about the Lumpkins. She usually perseverated for a few days before she decided how to express her sympathy. As she so rarely left the house now, attending the wake was out of the question. She decided to make some brownies and a casserole.

"Will you take them to the Lumpkin house?"

My blood suddenly boiled.

"Absolutely not! I am not taking them anything! He may have killed a girl!"

"Well, we don't know that for certain, do we? The children don't have a father."

"Then why did he take the big plunge? Mrs. Devoe lost her daughter, Mom. Rita and I went to the wake and up to their trailer. Larry Lumpkin was a fraud. I don't know what he did, but in the end, he deserted his family under the suspicion of murder. Think about it, Mom."

Her face drained with hurt. My mother looked away and left the room.

That night, I dreamed that I was at Smokey Hollow. *It is autumn and a chill has ridden in on the winds of a new season. A "Code Mountain-Top" has been called through the loudspeakers. This means that someone has gone missing. I am sent out from my ward to aid in the search. I meet up with another worker from a nearby ward.*

"Do you know who is missing?", I ask.

"Dunleavy. Never did know if he has a first name. We just call him Dunleavy."

We run and run, calling out his name, over and over. The gray autumn sky grows black. We scour the woods and the out buildings. I do a quick pass through of Dan's maintenance barn.

"Dunleavy! Dunleavy!"

All we can see now are juggling flashlights and the tiny lit ends of cigarettes.

"DUNLEAVY! DUNLEAVY!"

Somehow his name is separated for search purposes. It becomes two words, with heavy emphasis on the first.

"DUN-LEAVY! DUN-LEAVY!"

I hear the distant mournful cry of the 7:00 train, rolling through the Enchanted Mountains. The lonely sound becomes louder as the locomotive winds along the serpentine tracks. Strangely, the long warnings of the train join the cadence of our search cries.

There is a commotion up ahead. Dunleavy, panting and sweaty, sits in the dewy weeds. Randy, the night watchman, ties his hands behind him with strap restraints. Dunleavy is wincing and struggling to catch his breath. He desperately looks around for a way out. Instead, he is led away toward solitary confinement. He is limping and looks as if he has lost a shoe. Sadly, trying to protect his own dignity, he drags a wet pant leg along the road, marching off to his new cell. I blink myself awake.

CHAPTER ELEVEN

At Smokey Hollow, I was reassigned to a different ward. Someone had gone out with a back injury, so I replaced them in ward five. I viewed it as a conspiracy, but in retrospect it probably wasn't. The folks I cared for there were in adult cribs and quite physically involved. While the ward was quieter; I missed the activity of the kids. There was a great deal of hygiene, turning, and repositioning. The folks were prone to bedsores primarily because many of them could not shift around or move voluntarily. Just a pinprick of a mark could turn into a large ulceration quite quickly. So, we did what we could to prevent them. One of the residents had hydrocephalus, or water on the brain. While it was very difficult for Mark to move, he had a tremendous memory for music. He told me that he loved the soundtracks from *Hair* and *Jesus Christ, Superstar*. So, I brought them in and played them on an ancient turntable. He was ecstatic when he heard "Aquarius" and "Let the Sunshine In"! Mark told me that he wanted to start a new routine after lunch. He said that he wanted to get people moving. We got extra pillows so he could sit halfway up, and we let him use the megaphone from the emergency response closet.

"My friends, sit up and roll over. Wiggle your nose and your toes.

You will never see the light of day being weak and dependent! We must get stronger so we can take care of ourselves! Rise up, and roll over! You will only be imprisoned if you let yourself be treated that way!"

I was promptly written up on this ward, too, for "creating false hope and unauthorized use of emergency response equipment." The ward supervisor had heard the commotion of music and Coach Mark's barking orders, and that was it for those sessions. I continued to see Mark now and then and called him the "Minister of Inspiration and Advocacy"!

That summer, my brother, Kevy, came home. He had planned to seek spiritual guidance in Kathmandu but instead was bagging groceries at Big Al's Market. My Dad had refused to co-sign on a loan to get Kevy to Nepal.

"You can meet the Doiley Lamada, or whatever he is called, on your own dime. It won't hurt you to work at the grocery store for a few months."

"If you are referring to the Dalai Lama, he is from Tibet, not Nepal. He lives in India, though, due to the Chinese strangling of Tibet."

"Well, get yourself down to Big Al's. He will be expecting you."

To preserve family harmony, Kevy moved into Lorna's house until it could be readied for sale. I went to see him a few times. He told me that he had become a vegetarian. He told me he had been refining recipes involving lentils and chickpeas. Lorna's house, always an odd place, now had a combination curry powder/dog funk. To add to the confusion, Kevy burned odd sticks of incense while involved in meditation. He listened repeatedly to the music of George Harrison's "Concert for Bangladesh." He had posters of Ravi Shankar next to Lorna's figurines. He didn't socialize much and complained a great deal about working at Big Al's.

"Unhealthy people come in every day looking for bloody meats to fry or barbecue. They add potato chips, soda, or beer. And Big Al just serves it up. He exchanges beef hearts, tongues, and livers for cash. Americans are losing their strength because of their detestable diets."

"Do you want to grab a beer sometime, Kevy?"

"No. Alcohol poisons the spirit of the human soul. It makes people give into temptation. Kind people turn into junkyard dogs, and shy people embarrass themselves. It worms its way through their brains and destroys them."

"Kevy, I made some posters of Colleen, asking people to call the police if they know anything. Can you see if they can put some up at the store? Everybody in town goes to Big Al's."

"Good idea, there. But I am not sure Big Al will care. I will ask his wife, who runs the deli. Did the cops ever tell you anything?'

"Wally Banks didn't even know who we were. He had the wrong case file and started telling us about some other missing woman. It was totally lame."

"Well, this is no doubt part of a larger conspiracy or cover-up. You saw what happened to Richard Nixon. Don't think things like that aren't happening all around you!"

Frankly, Kevy was starting to scare me, so I left a few minutes later. He wished me Nirvana or Namaste or something like that.

Back at work, I was relieved to learn that I was returning to my ward. I had missed the kids and my friend Birdie. Vina, often reluctant to interact, seemed to be happy to see me. She pulled me toward the book rack as soon as she saw me. I read her two stories for good measure. I kept staring at her face, sensing a change. She yawned, and I finally saw that she had no teeth! When Birdie arrived, she told me that the dentist had diagnosed her with "advanced periodontal disease due to retardation."

"Oh come on, Birdie! Vina was wicked obsessive about her teeth. She loved toothpaste and if anything brushed her teeth too hard. She always had a foamy mouth at hygiene time."

"I know. I was just tellin' you what I was told."

"You know what? Vina tried to bite 'Vile Giles' when she was in here. That's why her teeth were pulled."

Birdie had a sudden epiphany.

"Wow, I think you are onto something. When I worked on ward two, Finnie Mae Patterson bit off half an ear one day. She went away for significant dental work. I never saw her again 'til I went to ward eight to pick up a shift. Her cheeks were all sunken in. She also had 'lost her voice.' Now back in the day, Finnie Mae would scream like a wildcat. She was so loud, they probably heard her in town. She had a large scar on her throat, too. Staff were told that she had infected teeth, which spread to her throat, but none of us believed it. She lost her teeth because she bit someone and her voice because she screamed!"

"Birdie, we need to find out what is going on around here. This place is really starting to creep me out. They are doing life-altering surgery for convenience? I am going to get some answers, and I don't care what happens!"

In July, at long last, the fair came to town. Rita and I decided to go together as my parents had declined. As they say in weather land, it was a "real scorcher." The temperature topped above 90. We went to all of the animal exhibits. We saw chickens in tiny cages, fluffing themselves up or screeching randomly. A loose turkey caused a near panic as it zig-zagged through a crowd from the Over 60 Club. All of the distinct animal odors grew more intense with the heat. Rita gagged in the pig barn, so we evacuated and got some lemonade. We ate slimy chili dogs followed by slabs of fruity taffy.

We drifted through the midway. We stopped to see the "Human Torch" eat fire. I told Rita that they should have named him "Kerosene Breath." "Señor Margarita" appeared as a bearded lady. She had a canned recording, asking these obscure questions:

"Should she go to the salon and let ladies coif her hair?

Or, should she smoke cigars and cuss in the barber's chair?"

As we exited the tent, I looked ahead to the next exhibit. My draw dropped, and I felt a sudden surge in blood pressure. I saw Polly. She wasn't there in person, but her picture was on a large canvas banner. She was part of a huge mural, a collective collage of people of all shapes and sizes. And she wore a strange crown on her head. Expecting to find her inside, I quickly paid my admission and ran in. There were displays of curiosities and a goat with four horns. But there were no other people. I was relieved to know that she wasn't part of the show but continued to wonder where she was. Was she traveling with a sideshow somewhere, the butt of teenage mockery? Was a carney her summer caretaker?

The next day, I was anxious to see Birdie. I told her what I had seen in the sideshow. Like she frequently did, Birdie told me to "simmer down!"

"Maybe she just looked like Polly. Maybe you saw what you wanted to see."

"You mean like a carnival illusion? I will pay for your admission if you want to see the picture."

"O.K., I will take you up on that. Can you go Saturday?"

"Yes, will do."

As I was leaving work, I ran into my friend Dan. He looked anxious to see me and cut me off with his riding mower.

"G-g-got news. S-S-Steiner will be g-g-g-gone all next week!"

"Perfect! See if you can score me a key to the file room. I'll pay you."

"Y-Y-Y-You ain't got to pay me. I will g-g-get what you n-n-n-need."

"Danno, these people need our help. That is the most important thing. I appreciate everything that you are doing."

With sweat dripping down from his tattered baseball cap, he handed me a fresh foxtail.

"Never c-c-could control you. Best we can do is t-t-t-tame you, like a c-c-c-cobra that g-g-goes back in the basket at n-n-n-night."

We laughed!

"Just one more thing, Danno. Can you explain the tunnels again?"

Smokey Hollow had been built over a complicated system of tunnels. They were almost labyrinthine in nature, so it was difficult to navigate them without a good working knowledge. The tunnels made it easy to move people from place to place or to the infirmary during the winter months. But they were dark and forbidding. Dan drew me a map to the best of his memory. He told me that the furthest tunnel went to the cemetery. There was a ramp that led from the morgue to the storm cellar door. He told me that this made dispatching the dead fairly easy and almost completely hidden.

"The little b-b-b-baby wit' no brain was l-l-l-lucky to get a shoe b-b-b-box. Most of them g-g-go into the g-g-g-ground in bags made in some of the w-w-w-wards."

CHAPTER TWELVE

An early thunderstorm left the summer air heavy. Menacing gray clouds, undecided about their intentions, moved quickly along the horizon. Birdie and I got an early start at the county fair. Another rambunctious shower drove us into the Gallery of Gardening. Prize-winning produce was proudly displayed. Birdie, who had quite a green thumb herself, talked to some of the farmers. She excitedly said that she had gotten some great new ideas for her pepper patch. At last, the rain let up. We wandered down the soggy midway. I deliberately didn't tell her when we had reached the display. I gave her a sideways glance when we were in front of the "World's Most Unusual Oddities." She recoiled and grabbed my arm.

"It is her! I can't believe it! Do you suppose Steiner sold them her picture?"

"I am not so sure that he hasn't sold her! We don't even know where she is!"

We paid for admission on the off chance that she was in there, but she wasn't. The same sad little goat blathered away! We went back out front. At the admission gate sat a heavily made up woman with a feathered hair comb in her hair. I remembered her stage name of "Lady

Lorelei, the world's most extraordinary contortionist." The highlight of her unusual performance was her nimble ability to comb her hair with her feet and insert her plumed hair accessory with her toes.

"Excuse us. There is a display behind you. Do you know any of those people? We think we recognize one of them."

She recited off some of the sideshow titles: "Slim Pickens," "Wild Gator Boy," Señor Margarita," and "Swamp Baby." I grabbed a nearby broom and pointed to Polly. With carney disinterest, she said, "no, that there is Juan Gabriel."

More confused, I asked if she knew where this Juan Gabriel was.

"What the hell, are you the cops or somethin'? Last time I seen him, he was in Pennsylvania tourin' with Johnny Lee Hager's show."

Birdie reassured me as she often did.

"Sure did look like her at first. There was a real resemblance. Sorry it didn't work out."

At Smokey Hollow, I had carefully thought out my plan. Dan had told me that the files were kept in a separate area outside of Steiner's opulent office. I was going to have to get past his secretary, Vera something-or-other. So, I had decided to toss a rock at a window near her desk. Drawn to the distraction, Vera would move away, and I would let myself in and lock the file room behind me. My strategy was to do this just before her shift ended at 5:00.

Things didn't go exactly as planned. I threw the rock a little too hard and shattered the window. Glass fell to the sidewalk below. Once I got inside the door, I heard Vera on the phone.

"Why yes, Officer Muskie, it was the strangest thing." And later, "No, I don't see anyone around. I do recall that Ronnie Ray Wettles used to break windows, but I don't know why he would have been out of the ward unsupervised."

I hid in the coat room while she wrapped up on the phone. In a change in my favor, she decided to go outside to meet Musty. She walked right past as I squatted under the coat rack. I breathed a sigh of relief and quickly let myself into the file room. I left the lights off and hid between the book racks. I had decided that I would remain there until I had been assured that Vera had left for the day. I had brought my camping flashlight so as not to draw attention to my deeds. I stared at the files. There they were. Just within my reach. Outside, I heard glass being swept up and later a bit of hammering. Vera came back in, did a bit of fussing here and there, and shut down the lights. I waited. Keys jangled at the exterior door. Faintly, I heard a car door shut and an engine rev up. It was time to go to work.

Much to my dismay, the files were organized in some kind of secret order. Three-digit numbers were followed by letters. So I randomly started rummaging through them. This was taking way too long! I was breathing heavily. My heart raced. There were no windows or obvious circulation in the room. I started to regret this whole scheme. What if there was nothing to find?

At last, under 707VH, I found my friend, Vina Howard. The first number was the number of the ward. I found Polly's ward, but nothing with a first initial "P." Was her file removed? Or hidden somewhere? I started opening every one of them. One had pages that were not closed on the rings, and everything drifted to the floor. I quickly picked that mess up and jammed the file back in. I thought I heard a noise outside. It sounded like a car door. It was getting hotter in the cramped room. Finally, I found Polly's photo in a file. Her beaming smile shone brightly in her photograph. The picture was eerily similar to the one at the fair. I took it and put it in my pocket. I looked at the identifying information and was stunned. Polly's given name was Juan Gabriel Principe! She had been born a boy. I went back to the photograph. It was the same person painted on the banner at the fair. "Juan Gabriel," as reported by Lady Lorelei. Steiner had no doubt sold the image to the carneys. My blood boiled.

Furiously, I paged to the medical section. I wrote down the term "estrogen" as Nurse Giles had signed for numerous injections. I remembered Lorna talking a lot about her estrogen imbalances, but I wasn't sure exactly what it was. There was an additional reference to a "previous orchiectomy," which I also copied down. In my sloppy agitation, I dropped the flashlight. One of the batteries became disengaged. It was pitch black. I was forced to turn on the light so I could fix it. The long fluorescent light blinked and hummed. This wasn't good. I fumbled around and reassembled my plastic light.

Shockingly, there was an abrupt banging at the door. I heard Musty. "Who goes there? Open this door at once!"

Fortunately, I had locked myself in, but I heard him with his gigantic key ring. He tried a few in the door. I had no choice. I inserted the skeleton key slowly and silently. And then, in a completely unanticipated moment, I pushed the door back with all my weight. Musty went right back with the door. I held it on him for good measure and quickly formulated my escape plan. I saw the door to the stairs to my right. I gave the door one last push, and Musty squirmed. And then, off I went! I ran faster than I had ever run in my life! I slammed the door to the stairs behind me. I found a trash can and put it behind it. I was looking for every possible way to delay him as I entered the tunnels. I heard him yelling behind me, but I had gotten quite a good jump start, and he seemed a safe distance back. I was totally out of breath by the time I reached the morgue. I opened the door to the cemetery ramp and tried the door to the outside. I felt a padlock flopping around, so that was not going to work! I should have checked this ahead of time! I was trapped! Quickly galloping back to the morgue, I dropped my flashlight on the way. I looked around. Musty was on the move, and I heard him closing in. I jumped into a bin that looked like one from the laundry building and covered up. Seconds later, Musty made it to the death chamber. From what I could hear, he was coughing and wheezing. I could smell him. Or, maybe it was the old laundry bin. I sensed him to be near the tunnel and suddenly remembered my stray flashlight. He seemed to be moving in that direction.

"Who goes there? Show yourself at once!"

I sprang out of the bin, pulled the tunnel door shut, and latched it! And just like that, Musty was trapped. The loathsome slug was snared in a dark, fetid tunnel. I ran the other way. The farther along I was, the more I enjoyed the fact that he was locked underground! I returned to the file room, straightened up, and shut down the lights. I locked up and left, moving slowly toward the maintenance barn so as not to create suspicion. It was late. My watch said 7:30. I made way home on my bike.

I became somewhat obsessed with the uncertainty of Musty's recognition of me. I was reassured by the fact that he never used my name or called me out specifically. I was disappointed with myself for not having used a disguise. While I had worn a baseball cap, there was nothing else to protect my identity. Of course, I hadn't known that he would have been there, but he had likely been paying closer attention because I had broken the window. The thoughts began to nag at me repeatedly. They wormed their way through all of my rational thinking. When I got home, I started to panic. I pictured the police carting me off in handcuffs to the county jail. I wondered about criminal charges. What were the possibilities? As an employee, I guess I wasn't trespassing, but I was loaned a borrowed key to a room I had never used. I had been "seeking information to help people" said the "good voice." But you "locked someone away under the earth" said the other voice. Oh well, surely Musty's family would be missing him. He would be found.

I didn't have to work the next day. While it was good to have time to process what I had done, there were times when I wanted to go up to Smokey Hollow to see if he was out. I was uncomfortable and agitated. I squirmed and shook. Dreadful thoughts gnawed at me all day. I went to the library. Verna Lou Vaughn greeted me with questions about my recent whereabouts at church events. I mumbled something inaudibly and asked where the medical books were located.

"Well, young man, they are just over there in the Dr. Elbert Steiner collection. He donated the solid maple table and chairs that you see there. He takes care of the wayward souls of Jesus Christ Almighty. He works the Lord's miracles on the mountaintop."

Verna Lou's praises for Steiner caused me a shameful wave of guilt and remorse. Was I wrong? What had I done? An orchiectomy, according to the Elbert Steiner collection, referred to a surgical procedure to stop the production of testosterone. Whatever the reason for this life-altering surgery, it appeared that Steiner was in the midst of transforming Polly's sex. She was his experiment! And when one had been capable of something like this, what else was possible? I became enraged. I left the library in a huff. I blew right past Verna Lou. While riding my ten-speed, I had a heart-pounding panic attack. It was difficult to regain my breath. I stopped and sat down on a curb in the center of town. My mind raced as quickly as my ticker. I tried to focus and calm down. A police car pulled up. I thought he was there to take me in. This was it.

"Are you doing OK there, young man?"

I nodded affirmatively.

"Do you need anything? Did you fall off the bike or something?"

I shook my head the other way. Like a trembling toddler, I was only able to respond with head gestures and guttural vocalizations. I walked to the gas station and got some water from the fountain. I collected my bike and went home. I hid in my room and decided to take a nap. Despite the summer heat, I pulled the bedspread tightly over my head. Like a kid playing tent under the dining room table, I felt safe there in the sweaty darkness.

Rita knocked on my door later and announced that dinner was ready. For some reason, we were eating outside at our warped old picnic table. We rarely ate there, and at least once a summer, the bench would tip over if someone stood up too abruptly. Dad was forever creating solutions to these accidents, but so far none of them had worked. There seemed to be newly bought grill accessories that I didn't recognize. Dad was preparing hot dogs, likely the easiest thing on earth to grill. But he carried on as he was known to do with complicated and contradictory grilling ideas. As usual, while he blathered on, he burned them to a blackened crisp. They grew large bubbles and eventually slit themselves wide open.

"OK, here we are now. Don't forget all the fixings!"

Mom turned to me and said, "You haven't mentioned much about your job lately. How is it going?"

"Oh, my God," I thought. "Does she know? Why is she asking this now? Are the police looking for me? Has she heard rumors in town?"

"It's OK. So, what can we do about looking for Colleen again? Has anyone heard anything?"

My efforts to change the subject were obviously awkward.

Dad began, "I had coffee with Detective Banks last week. He mentioned that the DiStefanos are moving away. Maybe that kid did have something to hide."

"The last time Rita and I went to see Banks, he knew nothing. He was reading from the wrong file. He told us more about the other case than our own sister."

"Well, he is the detective, not you two. Did it ever occur to you that they know more than you do?"

Rita spoke up. "There was never a shred of evidence that Joey did anything wrong. Can we ever stop blaming him?"

I followed. "I also think that we need to involve Kevy in this once in a while. While he is concerned, his mind seems to drift every now and then. Last time I saw him, he scared me."

With the familial rise in blood pressure and agitation, Mom indicated that she suddenly felt faint. She and Dad retreated to the house so they could finish their picnic in front of the fan. I am sure that Mom could not cope with the mention of Kevy, because she would have already noticed the changes that I had referred to. Rita and I were left to pick up the pieces of the only barbecue of the season.

"Every single time, Dad goes back to the DiStefanos. Broken record! Get over it! Move on!"

"I know. I guess they search for their truth as much as we want ours."

It was hard to believe that I had said something so rational. Usually the one to stir it up, I had somehow managed to calm things down.

My sister Rita was by far the most physically fit member of the family. Even when she was a toddler, I never heard her so much as whimper. She was a monster at our family badminton games, driving the birdie downward like a falcon chasing its prey. Four years my junior, Rita had always been the first one on the rope swing when we had snuck down to the Raccoon River. She would pull the rope briskly up to the highest possible point and set loose with all her might. She would fly across the river like a bird and suddenly spiral downward into the deep, cool river. As she sailed across the water, she cried out in a primitive screech, similar to an angry blue jay. She had begun to run track in her freshman year and gained a favorable reputation as a long-distance runner. As her training grew more rigorous, she eventually stopped our shared smoking. Thus ended our "smoke and swear" sessions, or, as she had called them, "cigs and cuss." While all of us kids enjoyed the spoils of Uncle Willie's taxidermy labors, Rita was the only one who would help with the painstaking removal of the hides and such. She seemed fascinated with internal organs and guts. The rest of us turned our noses up at the stench and unidentified bloody messes. But Rita would emerge from Willie's strange little shed with blood-stained rubber gloves and an enthusiastic smile.

Rita was far more studious and serious than the rest of us. When she wasn't running, she was reading. She seemed totally absorbed by poetry and always recited her new-found treasures. While she loved standard bearers such as Whitman, Dickinson, and Yeats, she frequently veered off course and read the likes of Anne Sexton, Adrienne Rich, and Leonard Cohen. She faithfully wore a bracelet for an American soldier, missing in action when his helicopter had been shot down over Laos. She had written many letters to former President Nixon when he was in office. She pleaded with him to end the war and find those who were missing or captured. After the war ended, she faithfully wrote to Souphanouvong, the leader of Laos, a few times a year. She wrote passionate and poignant letters in honor of the soldier whose name she wore. She kept a box of pre-addressed envelopes to the White House and would insert the name of the current Commander in Chief so that she was always ready to speak out against any conflict or crisis.

Rita babysat in her spare time. She often watched the Tremont triplets who lived down the street. Poor Mr. and Mrs. Tremont had run through most of the sitters in town, but it seemed that only Rita had the courage to return when called. She ruled the roost and ran a tight ship. Timmy and Tommy seemed fairly easy to manage, but brother Troy was another story. He displayed extended tantrums and was generally quite defiant. At age seven, Troy was more or less a larger version of a two-year-old who constantly said "no" and repeatedly teased and provoked the other two. In private, Rita referred to Troy as a "demonic psychopath." There were rumors in the neighborhood that he routinely killed frogs and toads. Troy was a problem, and Rita seemed to be among the few who could establish some rules. Mr. Tremont lavished her with extra cash just to keep her on the hook.

CHAPTER THIRTEEN

With a mixture of anxiety and excitement, I returned to work the following morning. I had wondered, about once every five minutes, if Musty had spent all night in his dark little cell. Had he fallen ill in the tunnel or died there? Would I be charged with murder? While I appreciated Danno's loyalty, I had wondered if he had told anyone else about my plans. In a small town, word travels. A gesture can become a verdict just as easily as a rumor becomes the truth.

I rode my bike toward the maintenance barn to see if I could find Dan. And there he was! No, not Dan but Musty! He was doing his little creeper ride in his cruiser. Ironically, our paths crossed at the very spot where ward four had tumbled down in flames the previous winter. Most of the building had been hauled away in dump trucks, but large chunks of the foundation remained, now home to weeds and sloppily thrown-up fences. It was the Smokey Hollow way of neglecting the obvious. While Steiner sold Polly's identity to carnies, he left unsafe and abandoned buildings throughout the grounds.

Musty looked at me, and I looked back, directly into the flash of his stupid sunglasses. I whispered to myself, "Enjoy the tunnel, did you?"

I found Dan gassing up the mowers.

"M-M-Morning. D-D-D-Did you g-g-get what you wanted?"

"I did, thank you. Dan, Polly was born a boy. Steiner turned him into a woman."

Dan blushed vividly and began sweating. He seemed like he couldn't speak at all. His mouth hung open. He was unable to utter a word.

"How long was Musty underground?"

"F-F-F-Five or t-t-ten minutes. He h-h-h-had his walkie-talkie. I guess he called R-R-Randy, the night watchman."

I was beyond angry!

"Five or ten minutes! What the hell! Does he know who did it?"

"N-N-Not sure. Randy just told me there was an in-in-intruder."

"Thank you, Danno. Good work!"

I was anxious to see Birdie, but I was increasingly paranoid. I thought that the ward might be recorded or monitored after my break-in. I whispered to her and told her to call me after work."

Just a few minutes after I got home, I heard the telephone. It was Birdie, but I had to talk in code because my mother kept wandering in and out of the room. She had answered the phone and was no doubt intrigued that I had a call from an older woman. After Birdie figured out what I meant about Polly, she asked about Colleen. She told me that she had mentioned her case to Mary McDougal who wrote for the *Enchanted Mountain Chronicle*. Apparently, this reporter indicated that she would be happy to write an article about Colleen to see if it helped gather new information. I called her the very next day. She asked me to come in and meet with her. She thought a photo of Colleen would help. The last class picture we have of Colleen was from her sophomore year. As I recall, she had hated the image, but I had little choice. I stared at the picture for a long time. It had been so long since I had seen her.

I was so eager to get Colleen's story out that I showed up twenty minutes early at the newspaper office. Mary was a fairly young-looking reporter and looked tiny behind her clumsy-looking electric typewriter.

She was very observant. While she took notes in her little spiral notebook, she thoughtfully looked at me throughout the interview. Emotionally, she seemed swept up in the story and appeared to tear up a bit now and then. I was profusely thankful as we concluded the interview. She promised she would have something in a few days. With one more glance, she said, "Is there something else you would like to tell me?"

I stood up and prepared to leave. I shook her hand. I turned to walk away. Suddenly, I reversed course. With trepidation and relief, I said, "Yes, there is something else I would like to tell you. If you have a few minutes, I would like to talk with you about my workplace, Smokey Hollow."

In just a few days, there was a pleading article about Colleen in the paper. It described her and asked for witnesses or information. Mary McDougal must have gone to the police demanding details. She provided Wally Banks's phone number. Colleen's picture was prominently displayed. Mom wept when I showed it to her.

Four weeks later, there was another article in the *Enchanted Mountain Chronicle*. The huge headline was stunning.

SHOCKING ALLEGATIONS AT SMOKEY HOLLOW

The Enchanted Mountain Chronicle has learned of graphic and disturbing charges made by employees at the sprawling Adult Care Facility located in Smokey Hollow. It has been alleged that experimental and unnecessary surgical procedures have been performed there routinely. In addition, vulnerable patients who have physical or mental disabilities have been overly medicated and subjected to degradation and cruelty, it is alleged. A suspicious fire on the grounds in February killed seven and injured nine of the residents. Previously thought to have been started by one of the residents, at least three staff members reported that they saw another employee flee the building before the alarm was pulled. Police are investigating, and an immediate evaluation of the care of the residents was ordered by officials in Albany. Elbert

Steiner, Superintendent of the facility, could not be reached for comment. His office reported that he was out of the country, speaking at a medical conference in Europe. *The Enchanted Mountain Chronicle* is committed to following this story, and further details about these allegations will appear in subsequent editions.

I was swept away by the reporting of Mary McDougal. She had conducted several clandestine interviews of concerned employees in a short amount of time. Her reporting was straightforward and direct. Instead of leading readers to a conclusion, she threw the questions into the air for the public to draw their own conclusions. Since there was no official denial from the institution, the townsfolk formed their own opinions. In a small town, rumors usually spread faster than a wind-fanned grass fire. Those with limited knowledge of such facilities regarded the story with disinterest. Friends and relatives of employees circled the wagons in their own attempts to justify the treatment of the residents of Smokey Hollow. The eyebrows of suspicion were raised whenever a new article appeared. Staff members at the facility turned on each other, never really knowing who had spoken to the reporter. There was a thick cloud of paranoia and doubt shadowing each day at work. A trio of three officials from Albany were sent in to guide the facility in the meantime. Two were social workers and the other was a nurse.

The first victim of the reporting was Velmajean. She was stripped of her supervisory status, removed from contact with the residents, and demoted to food service. She was forever wrapped tightly in her hair net, and her tortuous insults and taunting were gone. Her primary function in her new role was to gather up balls of food in an ice cream scoop.

I ran into Dan after an article about the February fire appeared.

"The p-p-police came right up h-h-here. They was asking all k-k-kinds of questions!"

"Good, Danno. Musty must be squirming like a worm too far from a puddle at this point!"

"H-H-Hey! Sounds l-l-l-like somethin' I w-w-would say!"

"Yeah, see what I get for hanging around you!"

"Well, least you ain't s-s-stammerin', y-y-yet!"

We laughed, giddy with a new-found credibility.

Through an attorney, Elbert Steiner reported that Smokey Hollow was a renowned training center for physicians. While numerous, life-saving procedures had been performed there, surgical residents had been involved in the diagnostics and actual surgeries. At four different points in the article, it was reiterated that Steiner was the superintendent, with very little time for day to day involvement with medical procedures. And, much to the dismay of many of us, the article mentioned that he was not a surgeon as we had always been told. Even though many of his speeches were about surgery, it appeared that he was crafting a much different story while he waited things out in Europe. When asked about the specific surgeries, he lashed out.

"These are absurd exaggerations created in the minds of completely hysterical, entry-level staff. Only members of our medical team have access to confidential health records. Obviously, these charges are the result of fertile imaginations, which are necessary when there is such limited knowledge of reality."

Little did he know that I had seen those records. And, in regard to the photograph, he seemed equally irate.

"A local photographer was hired to take annual pictures of our patients. I believe that they have since gone out of business. We made it clear to this firm that the confidentiality of our unfortunate residents was of utmost importance. However, we had no control over the use of the negatives. If they were sold to some sort of travelling group of charlatans, it would be a good example of the unscrupulous doing business with the deceitful."

I met with Mary McDougal a second time. Concerned that Polly had not come back to the hollow, I gave her as many details as I could. While we had been told that she was away visiting family, "Lady Lorelei" had given a much different report. I told Mary that she had been last seen, if indeed it was her, in Pennsylvania with a carnival directed by one Johnnie Lee Hager.

Two weeks later, Mary called me and asked if I could come back in again. After some exhaustive searching, she had located Johnnie Lee Hager in Florida. He was living in the town of Gibsonton and had recently retired to the carnival community there.

"Mr. Hager was happy that I had found him. He said that he had called Smokey Hollow several times and that no one ever returned those calls."

I shifted in my seat. Mary's voice was different. Something didn't feel right.

"What did he want?"

"He said that he had continued to receive bills for Polly's performances after the carnival had ended. Apparently, he received letters accompanying them written in a threatening tone."

"Where is she now?"

Mary's tone changed again.

"Sadly, she became ill in Pennsylvania and developed a terrible cough. Mr. Hager rushed her to a hospital in August but she had come down with pneumonia and died. He said that he had called his contact person at Smokey Hollow, Elmer Muskie. No one ever called him back despite his leaving urgent messages with the secretary."

I blinked away my anger and sadness.

"Oh, my God. Where is she then? Where did he leave her?"

"He said that he sent the carnival on to the next stop without him. He stayed two extra days and found a local cemetery for burial. He wasn't sure of the name of the county by he knew that it was near Harrisburg when all that happened. He had kept papers in case anyone was ever looking for her. He said that he would find them and give me the details. I am to call him again next week. I am so sorry for your loss."

"Thank you."

"And, there is just one more thing. He said that there was a small woman with a foul mouth who brought Polly to him for the summer. They came driven in an old ambulance by Elmer Muskie. And this wasn't the first person Muskie had sent to the carnival. Mr. Hager said that authorities in both Pennsylvania and New York are cooperatively conducting an investigation. In addition to providing room and board for Polly, Mr. Hager said that he was sending Smokey Hollow two hundred dollars a month for her performances. He also had one of the ladies in the knife-throwing exhibit to look after her. He was also looking for a letter that he said was signed by a doctor, Schweitzer or something like that, in which Polly (or Juan Gabriel) was referred to as 'indigent and legally incompetent.' If she was, then he couldn't understand why the facility hadn't provided a staff person to travel with her."

"Good questions! If you speak with him again, all I want to know is whether she was happy in the end."

CHAPTER FOURTEEN

I wasn't sure who else had talked with Mary McDougal, so I asked Dan to see what he could find out on the "Holler radar." He had later suggested that I try Dawnlea Reddington, who worked on ward five. He reported that Dawnlea had been an outspoken advocate for the residents and that she had sounded pretty fed up with the infirmary. Dawnlea agreed to meet me and suggested a shelter at the Racoon River Park. We couldn't risk being seen in town with everything hitting the newspaper.

Dan issued a warning, "D-D-D- Dawnlea likes to t-t-t-talk!"

Dawnlea was eager to talk to me while she chain smoked. She seemed agitated, and her quick green eyes darted about as if she were on the run from everyone. She wore a Black Bear Campground sweatshirt, but the two Bs had worn off so it said, "lack ear Campground" instead. Her sweatshirt wore a layer of dog or cat hair. She nervously started speaking.

"We've been having all kinds of issues, and they just keep getting worse. Every day, I wonder if it will be my last day. We get no support from nursing. Nurse Giles treats us like we have the plague. We can't stand her!"

"Agreed. She is among the worst!"

"Last month, we lost Gustaf Fredrikson. He was one of our older residents but seemed in good health. He was an energetic Swedish man whose head had seen the wrong end of a fishing boat anchor when he was younger. He loved to speak in his native tongue and told me, 'vi ses snart,' whenever my shift ended. I think it means 'see you soon' or something like that. He spoke in both languages about conspiracies. He pledged allegiance to the Swedish King in his nightly prayers. He taught me all about the Swedish foods. I told him I didn't care for fish and seafood, but he went on and on about the herring and some kind of 'temptations' that were full of potatoes and anchovies. He told me how wonderful the house would smell after his mother would make some kind of saffron buns with raisins for the feast of Saint Lucia. He teared up when he talked about his mother. Sometimes, his voice would change a bit and he would tell me all about the evil spirits who roamed in the last month of the year. He had been told as a child that it was best to stay home through the whole month of December, so the trolls and the witches couldn't snatch you up. He looked like Santa Claus himself, and I don't think he ever hurt a single soul."

"What happened?"

"Oh, yeah. So, Steiner had put Gustaf on some new medication. We were told that he had some kind of dementia or something. But he was the same old 'Gus' to us. We thought the whole thing was strange because we had to take him to the infirmary for his injections while the other medications were given on the ward. Nurse Giles usually gave him the shots, so he hated them more and more. He got worse each time. It was awful. He started to slur and slobber. He had trouble walking back. He stumbled and fell. We had to use a wheelchair. He started drooling all the time and could barely swallow his food. One day, Jerry Connors, an aide on the ward, found him stone cold dead. He was curled up in a ball on the floor in a puddle of pee. Musty swooped in after we called the infirmary and rolled him on to a gurney. He covered him up and wheeled him away. We never heard another word about it.

My cousin Lester Laforte is the cleanin' man up at the infirmary. I had asked him to snoop around a bit after one of Gustaf's injections. Best he could tell, he found vials of some kind of barbiturates. You know, like sedatives? While Lester was snoopin' he found a folder plain as day that said something about the use of barbiturates in dog 'euthro'… you know, when they put dogs to sleep? What is it?"

"Euthanasia?"

"Yeah, that's it!"

"Well, did you call the police?"

"No. Hell, Jerry told me we'd probably get fired if Steiner found out. I got a son to feed and can't lose my job."

"If you think someone was murdered, you should go to the police. Otherwise, nothing is ever going to change!"

"That ain't all. We almost lost Ronnie Ray Wettles a few months back. He's got some kinda obsession with glass. He has broken windows and mirrors whenever he gets the chance. He is always put in a straight-jacket and shipped off to solitary for a few weeks, but it don't change anything. Ronnie Ray has had more stitches and staples than anyone in the Holler. Despite all he done, we all love Ronnie Ray. He's got a real charm about him."

"So, what happened?"

"Well, after a shower, he slipped away and cracked a mirror. He slashed his own arm and cut an artery. He bled all over. Jerry Connors made a tourniquet with his leather belt, and we got him to the infirmary. There was Nurse Giles. She said that she was on lunch break and asked us to wait outside until she was done. Honest to God! Jerry was sweating and red-faced. He told her that we weren't going anywhere until we got the poor guy some help. Poor Ronnie Ray looked like all of his blood had been pumped out of him. Pale and weak, he laid his head on my shoulder and moaned. And all the while Giles sat there munching and crunching. She shifted her chair so she didn't have to see us. She chewed on saltine crackers covered with some stinky egg salad. Then she chomped on carrot sticks. To top it off, she took out one of those extra-long cigarettes, a Bronson and Hedges or whatever they are called. Jerry was cursing under his breath while she took long, deep drags. And get this: she didn't help us anyway! She called someone else when her lunch ended. It was unreal! She barked at the other nurse who came to help. She screamed that we would all be written up for taking a bleeding patient into the staff lounge. She pointed her finger in Ronnie's face and said that she would make sure he sat in solitary for a long time."

"And you told this to Mary from the newspaper?"

"Yes, I did. And I told Vera, my grandmother's sister-in-law. She works in Steiner's office."

Dawnlea abruptly looked at her watch and announced that she had to pick up her son at the babysitter. My head was literally spinning with these tales. I thanked her, hopped on my bike, and took a long ride along the Raccoon River. It was a gorgeous day in which the summer met fall. Leaves had already started turning, but Indian summer had warmed the spectacular foliage up. The country smell of burning leaves brought a primitive feeling to the woods. My thoughts raced. I tried to picture the events that she had described, but it was too much.

I rode my bicycle with newfound abandon. And I had a deepened respect for Mary McDougal and her ability to weave this incredible collection of stories into a straightforward, credible newspaper article. I pedaled through the streets and looked up at Smokey Hollow. The wall that surrounded it was about to come down, I thought. I was excited that the truth would come out.

In my dream, we are unleashed on Halloween. Too old for cheap plastic masks and trolling for candy, we are in that "in between" teenage phase. While we miss being cute kids, we have to appear as though Halloween means nothing. Armed with bars of soap and rolls of toilet paper, we venture forth. Colleen, Joey, and I are wandering aimlessly. At times, we duck behind trees and make random sinister noises. Unsure children scream or slowly change course so as not to appear frightened. We soap up Nettie Walters' windows because she had promised Colleen she would donate to the March of Dimes. When Colleen went to collect, Nettie told her that she never said any such thing.

We make our way to the Lumpkin house, a perfect little Cape Cod–style home. Their decorations are strictly autumnal. Calico corn hangs on the door and there is a large cornucopia filled with pumpkins and gourds. Cornstalks frame the front door. There is a bowl of apples and boxes of raisins with a small sign written in crayon that says, "May the Lord bless you with a bountiful harvest—please help yourself!"

We commit several rolls of toilet paper to our project. We toss it through trees and bushes. Joey gets serious and shimmies up the wrought iron. He puts several rolls in the gutters and we pull them down at random lengths. They blow back and forth lazily. With a soaking rain expected later, the property should be a fine mess for the Lumpkins to clean up on All Souls Day.

Meanwhile, Colleen is adding creativity to the squash harvest. With a magic marker from her tie-dyed bag, she is busy making evil faces on the round little Lumpkin pumpkins. She has emptied out the cornucopia and turns it over to resemble the shape of a witch hat. She draws on the little gourds, turning them into various animals. She sticks the gourds in window wells and the crooks of the smaller trees.

Colleen, Joey, and I are smoking cigarettes across the street as we admire our devilish creation. Distracted by the mess, we don't immediately notice the foursome approaching from the right. Joey suddenly pulls us behind a clump of bushes. Here they come! The Lumpkins! Larry is dressed as the tin woodsman, sparkling in silver and walking awkwardly as if his cardboard and tinfoil costume is cutting off his circulation. Faith is Glinda the Good Witch, complete with a crown and magic wand. Little Simon is struggling as the lion in a costume that looks homemade and oversized. Magdalena is Dorothy and carries a basket bearing a stuffed-animal dog and overflowing with fruit. No doubt they went to the apple bobbing event at the church.

Faith gasps as she looks toward their house. Larry drops to one knee, and the rest of the family performs simultaneous genuflection. Larry leads them in an immediate "prayer of forgiveness."

"*Lord Jesus, forgive these sad lost souls who have chosen the path of darkness. They know not what they have done. Like wayward sheep that stray from the flock, they will wander until they find You and You alone!*"

We continue moving silently into the pitch-black night while they pray for us.

"*Jesus, offer them a candle to bring them out into Your light. One day, they will find Your love.*"

At last, we are out of range and turn down a side street. Colleen giggles and does a loud sheep impression, "Baaaaah, baaaaah!"

We laugh and laugh. I awaken.

CHAPTER FIFTEEN

Uncle Willie invited me up to his ranch for his signature macaroni and cheese. He seemed to be branching out a little bit and had developed a new version with tabasco sauce. He had a new item in his taxidermy collection, a gorgeous gray lynx. With its huge pointed ears sitting high on its head, he referred to it as, "an owl in cats clothing."

"Seen the paper the other day. Was that you talkin' with the news?"

Nervously, I looked away.

"A lot of people were interviewed, so I am not exactly sure what parts of the story came from who."

"Oh, come on! Nothin' to be 'shamed of. You should be proud if you was defendin' those kids."

"Well, not everyone is going to see it that way."

"So what? We ain't put on this earth to try to please everyone. Sounds like there are some real polecats workin' there, treatin' those poor people like animals. Is Velmajean Crandall still workin' there?"

"Yes, she has a different last name now. She is one of the worst!"

"Ain't no surprise there. Her daddy was a low life. I think he whupped his kids every day of the week. They came to school with patched up clothes and black eyes, but everyone in town looked the other way. I think they was all afraid of the stinkin' old man. I heard it told that he kept a loaded shotgun on the kitchen table and would lay a few slugs up into the ceiling if the kids acted up at dinner. The church took up a collection for the family after their little daughter Cora Mae slid into the frigid Raccoon River on a pink plastic sled gone too far. Some in town said that he took the money and spent it all on a drinking binge at Tipsies. All the while he was tellin' his grieving story while chasin' teenage girls. Soon after, he was gone. Just like that. Family said he'd run off, but rumor was that there was a fresh-dug mound of dirt behind their outhouse. No one bothered to go up there to find out."

"Why do people do what they do to each other?"

"Don't ask me! I always thought that animals are more predictable. Except for cats."

I told Uncle Willie about Polly. He remembered her from the brief service we had for little Milkweed. He told me that he had some business to tend to in Pennsylvania and he would be happy to take me there if we found out where she was buried. At last, I was revved up again!

We packed up Uncle Willie's pick-up truck and left town. Dad was worried that we would be left in the hands of his half-brother, and Mom was generally sad about everything. It was about a four-hour trip through the Commonwealth so we decided to camp out to break up the trip. Willie drove, Rita rode in the middle, and I was in charge of the cassette tapes on the right. We were shoulder to shoulder, amid Willie's tools, receipts, and food wrappers. Uncle Willie spied a freshly struck deer, but we managed to distract him from stopping to see if he could use it for something.

Somewhere outside the town of Sinnemahoning, Willie pulled off into a scenic overlook. He said that he had some bartering to do. His plan was to drop me off at the local supermarket and I would get some food for our camp out. He and Rita would tend to taxidermy supplies or whatever they were doing. Then they would drive back and retrieve me. I made a grocery list on an old lunch bag. I prowled around the

Sinnemohoning Superette for about twenty minutes, collecting things that were easy to prepare. Willie claimed he had everything we needed in the truck, but finding them in the dark woods might have been a challenge.

The pick-up returned at the appointed time, and I stashed the grocery bags. Rita had a Styrofoam cooler at her feet. In ignorance, I asked for a drink. She quickly opened the cooler and pulled out some kind of frozen bird. She tried manipulating it as if it were attacking my face but it was frozen solid, so there was little animation left within it. Just as she pretended it was pecking my cheek, the truck hit a pothole and the beak left a bloody mark.

Uncle Willie said, "Suck it up, soldier. Your sister groused you!"

With wounded pride, I aimed for a snappy comeback.

"My sister has been grousing since the day she was born!"

Rita then proudly displayed her frozen collection of grouse and ring-necked pheasants. I did my best to express my clear disinterest.

We set up camp in Bald Eagle National Forest. I gathered some rocks to create a second fire pit. The autumn air had a bit of a sting to it so we wanted a second source of heat. Somehow, Uncle Willie managed to find a grill grate in the bed of his pick-up. We built a smaller fire for cooking and a larger one at the opposite end. We fired up some twigs and dryer lint that Willie also found in his truck! Once the logs caught fire, we seared some hamburger patties. I heated some canned spaghetti products, and we shared globs of those with each other. Rita indicated that her burger was not going to work without catsup. Obviously, my shopping skills required refinement. Without batting an eye, Willie walked over to the truck and somewhere in the overflowing glove-box, he found some little restaurant catsup packets. Beer washed it all down. My uncle indicated that his strategy for the next day would be to take our tents down early and dry them out in the truck bed and we'd drive on. He said that we would stop somewhere along the way to get breakfast.

Johnnie Lee Hager had told Mary McDougal that Polly had been buried in a potter's field in Dauphin County. Willie said we'd get there early the next morning. Mary had also meticulously written down his response in regard to Polly's "performances."

"Well, we didn't know what to do with her when she first joined our show. One day, I seen her go happy nuts when she heard a song by those Jackson kids. Of course, she rocked like an earthquake so we called the act 'Rock Around the Clock.' That was it. She seemed happy when the music started and never once got sick with all the spinning and rocking around. She never gave me no trouble at all. If anyone made a mockery of her, we threw them out. The crowds loved her."

A dewy day followed with those early morning tenting moments when there is denial that one must get up. I buried myself deeper into the flannel comfort of my sleeping bag. Eventually, I rose. Willie and Rita were waiting, so we packed up quickly. Rita and I grabbed a bucket from the truck to make sure the fires were fully extinguished. We stopped at the Maple Palace for breakfast. The diner had a fine buttery bacon aroma. We worshipped our mugs of coffee and dove into our platters of pancakes.

The spectacular fall colors were strikingly vivid as we neared Dauphin County. We stopped for gas. Directions to the remote cemetery were harder to come by. The gas station attendant had to call his father to get the exact location. When we finally found it, I took a deep breath and felt an incredible sense of relief. We found the most recently dug anonymous grave. I sat down in the grass. Rita had framed a picture of the Jackson Five taken from a teen magazine. She made a wreath of dried flowers and laid that on the grave under the photo.

I took a small envelope out of my pocket. I shook out some milkweed seeds, complete with their feathery little appendages that carry them airborne. I gave some to Uncle Willie and Rita. On the count of three, we blew them into the air, hoping that a few of them would sprout the following spring.

EPILOGUE

June 1979

While our beautiful Colleen is still missing, our family has joined with several others in New York and Pennsylvania and formed a group called "Beacon of Hope." Mary McDougal has been a great help by linking several newspapers. Essentially, whenever a person under twenty-one goes missing, the cooperating papers notify each other and Mary, who then passes the information on to the beacon families. Those who are able immediately go to help the families of the missing. We help with search efforts, babysit their other children, and run simple errands. With flashlights, we scour ravines and river beds. By daylight, we walk in grids through cornfields and campgrounds. Rita and I have participated in some of the searches. Dad, Birdie, and Mary McDougal helped with one in which a toddler was suddenly gone from her yard. Sometimes, the missing are discovered to have run away. We have found many clues. Beacon families sadly found the body of a missing thirteen-year-old girl from Allegany County.

My Mom has never been quite the same. Whenever she hears a car door open or shut, she quickly moves to the living room window.

It doesn't matter where the car stops or who is in it. She instinctively goes to the window and looks out each time. Her waiting seems so cruelly and eternally unanswered. Her laughter is rarely heard now. If she does laugh, she seems awkwardly embarrassed by herself, as if it should not be happening. Then she usually retreats to her room. If a car door shuts, she is instantly back at the window. And so it goes. Like a mother bird whose egg has fallen, she keeps the nest clean and warm, waiting anxiously for the nightmare to end. Occasionally she gardens. She digs holes and covers them back up without explanation. Many of her plants have died from neglect. Other weeds have encroached and taken over.

Dad, once a firm-jawed, well-dressed salesman, has become a much sloppier version of his former self. He broods in ways different from my mother. He hides in the flickering shadow of the television while gutters leak and faucets drip. My parents decided to "get away" on a brief vacation to Buttercup Lake. They had rented a cabin for four nights but were home the next day. He said that my mother was bothered by mosquitoes. She said that he was unaware that there was no television in the cabin. In truth, they had become incapable of experiencing pleasure outside of their habitual routines. With their beautiful daughter gone, they do their best to put on the mask of the living. Their eternal grief is their unity.

As a family, Colleen's absence has torn us apart. With Beacon, it has drawn us back together in fleeting moments. We do it all for Colleen, wherever she is. And, the families that we have helped in her honor are infinitely appreciative. Our never-ending pain has occasionally been channeled into comfort for others. Colleen would have wanted it that way. It is becoming harder to remember her now. She wasn't one for appearing in a lot of photographs.

"I prefer to remember moments in my own mind," she said. "Then, if I need to change the script a bit, I can."

Following his quick dismissal from Big Al's Market, my brother Kevy announced that he needed some time to "find himself." Al had told my Dad that Kevy had replaced all of the signs around the meat counters that advertised the specials. He had written other messages such as "Big Al is a Cow Killer!" and "Only Murderers Eat Meat!" We later found out that Kevy had also flunked out of college.

Kevy landed in a Hare Krishna community somewhere outside of New Orleans. The return address on the envelope indicated that it had come from Mississippi, but it was likely that New Orleans sounded like a more intriguing destination. He wrote me a long letter and made it clear that he had changed his name to Sadarshiv. He said that he is productively engaged in farming at the commune. He sent a detailed description of the fruits, flowers, and vegetables that he is tending. Apparently, the farm has several cows. He enjoys working with them and has taught all new recruits how to treat them in a humane manner. He meditates daily. He said that he looks forward to the day when I will join him on the path to fulfillment. And if I know anyone else whose heart is empty or seeking spiritual enlightenment, the commune is always open to them.

Rita has taken a part-time job at a veterinary clinic while she finishes high school. She seems to have a natural affinity for all the critters that come in sick or crippled up by unfortunate encounters with cars. She plans to apply to college at Cornell when she graduates. In whatever free time she has, Uncle Willie has been teaching her the fine art of animal rehabilitation and preservation through taxidermy. Her first finished product was a grouse, which she named after me.

My lifelong friend, Donnie Wayne Briggs, was elected as the youngest mayor of our town in history! He has initiated "Red, White and Blue Week" in June, which raises money for the fire department. There is a patriotic parade and a pancake breakfast. The town puts on a Betsy Ross Pageant and serves "Yankee Doodle Noodles and Ham" at the Methodist Church. He has gained some weight and exchanged his black concert tee-shirts for dull striped ties. While we still enjoy our chats, I hear far less gossip since his political advancement. He did call me with news about the late Larry Lumpkin. It turns out that the witness who said they saw Larry's car near the location of Dorena Devoe's body had recanted, so there was no conclusive evidence tying him to Dorena's disappearance. While the townsfolk had already convicted him in the court of popular opinion, I shivered with a twinge of sadness for his surviving family. Their lives were forever changed as well, and they eventually relocated due to the persistent rumors.

There are ongoing changes at Smokey Hollow. New people have been sent in on quality missions, but it has been very difficult to change the fundamental culture of the facility. The new people leave as quickly as they arrive. I have been sent to some of the other wards to help the employees view the residents as people. While that sounds very basic, the long-standing view has been that the residents are somehow lesser in value. While all of these changes and ideas float around, the needs of all those who live there are still present each day, making it difficult to take a genuine breath and formulate a sensible plan to free them of the institutional yoke.

Birdie's sister Robin had continued to decline in health and became bedridden. Birdie took several weeks off from work while her sister lay dying. I helped her plant a little memorial garden in her yard after Robin was buried. To be honest, Birdie has never been quite the same since her sister's death. She seems perpetually distracted and often looks away when talking to others. Her voice, once reassuring, seems on the edge of dread and worry.

The children, who were not supposed to be living at the facility by regulation, are being dispersed to other facilities. We said goodbye to Gary. He moved into a family care situation. We were happy to hear that he was going to get a new wheelchair and some adaptive equipment. I told his caseworker that we had been teaching him to be more independent with feeding, so they scheduled immediate therapy evaluations. Vina was still with us. Birdie and I knew that she would be more difficult to place. If anything, she kept things familiar to us in the midst of all the changes. We likely needed her more than she needed us.

Many of the adult residents are being moved into group homes. Some of the transitions are seamless, while others require more support. It is difficult for people who suffered years of ridiculous regimentation to adapt to a new world with rights and choices. Occasionally, I would run into them in the community shopping or at town events. It was so refreshing to see them off the mountain top, free of Smokey Hollow.

Danno told me that he had heard that charges are pending against Musty and Velmajean. With the cloud of the fire also hanging over his head, it was reported that Musty had mysteriously "retired." As no one in town has seen him for a few weeks now, Commander Briggs was dispatched to his mobile home. He told his son Donnie Wayne that the trailer smelled sour and was littered with copies of the local paper, each containing articles about the Smokey Hollow controversies. Long-neglected ashtrays sat near each of the newspapers. The elder Briggs said that he was surprised that the whole place hadn't gone up in flames. How ironic that it hadn't. Nothing suspicious was found at the residence, so it is presumed that he is out of town.

I saw Danno and told him, "I think Musty should have been named Musky, after a muskrat. My uncle used to take me to sit and watch them. They don't possess the elaborate elegance of a beaver. Their coats are nice and warm, but they are often hiding in the cold river mud. They smell, and they have a rat's tail. When the going gets tough, they dive and hide, just like he is right now. And they are quite good at finding a way out, just like he did in the tunnel. He'll come back, and he will pay for what he has done!"

"That's my b-b-buddy. All w-w-worked up again!"

Steiner is still hiding like a little mole in Europe. In essence, he sold out Musty and Velmajean as easily as Polly had been dispatched to the carnival. So, it appeared for a while that Velmajean may be the sacrificial lamb and the only person to answer for all of the Smokey Hollow abuses.

Just last month, Vera, the administrative secretary in the main office, also decided to retire. Before she did, she apparently called my friend Mary McDougal. Soon after, three police cars were seen parked under Steiner's vacated office. Officers were seen removing several boxes. In a couple of days, the *Enchanted Mountain Chronicle* was capped with a new headline.

NEW ALLEGATIONS OF MEDICAL MISTREATMENT AT SMOKEY HOLLOW

BOXES OF HIDDEN DOCUMENTS IN POLICE CUSTODY

As of today, extradition procedures are being pursued for Elbert Steiner. French officials are in agreement that he should be returned to the United States.

Perhaps one day soon, he will face a more uncertain legacy.

ACKNOWLEDGEMENTS

Thank you to People Inc. and the Museum of disABILITY History, especially Rhonda Frederick and Nancy Palumbo, for this opportunity.

I am appreciative to Carole Southwood, Rachel Bridges and Julia Lavarnway for their support in the development of this publication.

Thank you to my family, Roberta, Max, Eli, India and Eden. Your patience and support have allowed me to create this.

I also want to acknowledge Cynthia Nodland, Dr. Robert Neumann, Tina Squyres- Price, Lynn Bergreen and, the late Beth Nannen Foster. Each of you played an important role in the development of Smokey Hollow.

Books in Abandoned History Series:

On the Edge of Town: Almshouses of Western New York by Lynn S. Beman and Elizabeth Marotta

Dr. Skinner's Remarkable School for "Colored Deaf, Dumb, and Blind Children" 1857 – 1860
by James M. Boles, EdD, and Michael Boston, PhD

When There Were Poorhouses: Early Care in Rural New York 1808 – 1950
by James M. Boles, EdD

An Introduction to the British Invalid Carriage 1850 – 1978 by Stuart Cyphus

Abandoned Asylums of New England
A Photographic Journey by John Gray
Historical Insight by the Museum of disABILITY History

No Offense Intended: A Directory of Historical Disability Terms
by Natalie Kirisits, Douglas Platt and Thomas Stearns

The Gold Cure Institutes of Niagara Falls, New York 1890s by James M. Boles, EdD

Of Grave Importance: The Restoration of Institutional Cemeteries by David Mack-Hardiman

They Did No Harm: Alternative Medicine in Niagara Falls, NY 1830–1930
by James M. Boles, EdD

Path to the Institution: The New York State Asylum for Idiots by Thomas E. Stearns

The Magic Fire: The Story of Camp Cornplanter by David Mack-Hardiman

Buffalo State Hospital: A History of the Institution in Light and Shadow
A Photographic Journey by Ian Ference
Historical Insight by the Museum of disABILITY History

*Beautiful Children: The Story of the Elm Hill School and Home for Feebleminded
Children and Youth* by Diana M. Katovitch

J.N. Adam Memorial Hospital: Her Inside Voice by Char Szabo-Perricelli

---

Reprints from the Museum of disABILITY History Collection:

The Education of the Feeble-Minded by Kate Gannet Wells, Introduction by Douglas Platt

The Perkins Institution and Massachusetts School for the Blind
by Samuel Eliot, Introduction by Douglas Platt

*A Poorhouse Trilogy: Questions Relating to Poorhouses, Hospitals and Insane Asylums (1874);
Handbook for Visitors to the Poorhouse (1888); He's Only a Pauper, Whom Nobody Owns! (1910)*
Reprints from the Museum of disABILITY History Collection, Introduction by Douglas Farley

CPSIA information can be obtained
at www.ICGtesting.com
Printed in the USA
BVOW11s1957220917

495622BV00011B/192/P